HOW WE STOPPED TIME

NAYAN BRAMHANWADE

Contents

PREFACE

Standing out is the imagination that leads to the story's ideas. The book is a sincere narrative of a time-travelling journey where fantasy adds to it too. I can say that I have always wanted to create a narrative that defies time in such a way that readers will feel they are travelling along with characters that carry out their journeys through various stages of life. This story is inspired not just by my affinity for the genre but by the countless precious moments spent with my friends. Similarly, a lot of incidents recorded in the book are similar to our acts, showing the point of friendship and the bonds we have created in all these years. Although I cannot say for sure that one day I will create a masterpiece that will surpass this book, it is very close to my heart. My passion was broken with the efforts, and fun was for sure there as I strived to build a world that every reader could easily dive into. Each page is filled with exploring and the joy of adventure, where the readers can join me in this wonderful writing journey. This story is not only a plot; it is a celebration of creativity and the magic of storytelling. It explores not only time but also the ties we make along the way. To travel this path with you, my reader will make it worthwhile for both of us. And, above all, it is a celebration of imagination, friendship, and the endless adventures that come our way.

Acknowledgements

There is a reason why I wrote this book. It is inextricably linked to the priceless support of my friends during a difficult time. Their unwavering support made the abstract notion of wanting to write a story that would stick with people feel less ephemeral, and more like a physical reality. I wanted to write fiction for years, but struggled to figure out how to even start writing something that I felt was worth reading. And then one afternoon, with my friends rallying around me in faith that I had something to say, I picked up a pen. But this memoir is not just that. It is a representation of the bond I share with my friends.

The female characters I created in my story emulate people I know personally, their unique, basic characteristics and personalities expressed in a fiction narrative. Each female character serves a memo to my friends. Each has the strength and fortitude of the friends who believed in me when I wanted to give up. These friends have generously supported me through thick and thin and perhaps brightened my days throughout college. I insert their essence in the pages of this book to highlight their contributions and contributions to my life experiences throughout our stories from meaningful moments.

In this narrative, I hope to explicitly portray friendship, persistence, and the beauty of storytelling. The characters will muddle through the unforeseeable challenges that often occur in life while implementing the lessons from my life, to be encouraging during one's actions of self-discovery and self-growth. The stories of these coincidences will all intertwine to show how friendships can bring illuminance to the dreariest paths.

ACKNOWLEDGEMENTS

Overall, this narrative serves as an example of friendship, and how is it all a matter of time before we offer up our own. I hope to inspire everyone to think about some of their friendships, and the moments that changed the relationship. As for me, every time I put my life experience to fiction, I at least hope to inspire someone to think of their own stories, and remember that their stories are all worth telling.

I
Cafe-one

Morning broke fresh, and Vrushabh wakes up with a great unwillingness to give up the sweet comfort of his bed. The day was wholly overcast, so the city was put up in a sorry mood. This, however, did not deter Vrushabh from his routine drive to college. That day, of course, fate had other plans for him. He reached the bus stop helplessly, where the mist of the rain caused him to miss his bus. At that moment, the drizzle had turned into a torrential downpour with thunder. He rushed inside the open door of a cafe, and that cafe was Cafe-One.

As Vrushabh entered the cafe, his eyes fell on a girl seated in a wheelchair. She seemed to be the same age as him. The rest of the cafe lay deserted, save for these two people. Vrushabh sat down on a chair beside the girl, who immediately looked at him with curious eyes.

Vrushabh furrowed his brow.

"Is everything alright, miss?"

She answered, mischief glistening in her eyes, "Everything's just perfect, sir. Would you care for a cup of coffee?"

Vrushabh nodded, "Yes, please, with two sugars."

He said, "Yes, two, please." She replied, "Coming right up," turned around, and

Vrushabh asked,

"By the way, what's your name?"

"Sharvari," she replied, in a murmur, with a smiling face, as she proceeded to make the coffee efficiently at the counter.

While Sharvari Was engrossed in the preparation of coffee, Vrushabh looked around and was lost in some thoughts. He kept on staring at the lavish design and impeccable decor of the place. ``How I was out of my senses to have not known about this place in the area," he pondered.

``Does she come here occasionally to fill in for someone, or does she work here?" he enquired Sharvari.

Sharvari, when asked, looked at him with an amused expression and replied: "I am the owner of this place".

This was a surprise to Vrushabh, who burst out:

"It can't be at "

Sharvari just said: "Believe it or not. Both amount to the same thing."

She gave him the cup of coffee that she had just then brewed. Pointing at his college uniform, she asked, at first:

"Aren't you going to classes?"

"Caught in the rain," replied Vrushabh casually.

What would be just a casual meeting soon evolved into an engrossing talk between the two, something that later on would transform both their lives.

Just when the two of them were having a good chat, their evening in the café was disrupted by the loud scraping sound of a pitch-black sedan crashing into the parking lot.

Vrushabh and Sharvari both rushed in the direction of the banging sound, startled by the unexpected collision. As Sharvari went to push the door open, all of a sudden, her movement stopped, and she told Vrushabh to stop. In a gush of haste, she asked him to find her a place to hide. Puzzled,

Vrushabh inquired, "What's wrong?"

to which Sharvari looked at him with a pleading expression, "Please, just trust me."

Vrushabh quickly took charge and wheeled Sharvari toward the back of the café, opposite the counter and in the direction of the storage area. Inside, they ducked into the storage room behind the clanging door.

From their concealed vantage point they watched the doors of the crumpled sedan open. Three men and a lady came out, the men gesturing to the lady as she walked towards the door of the cafe.

As the group entered, they started to look frantically at the cafe with urgency and determination; she sat on a comfortable couch.

The gang of burglars searched through every nook and corner of the coffee shop but found nothing, having wasted fifteen minutes. Their frustration and patience were slowly creeping across their faces when the cold leader of the gang, a commanding woman, rose from the couch. She had a word with the men, in a deceptively calming tone that belied her cold-blooded personality:

"Hear me out. We need a package, and I don't have time for all this nonsense. Find it fast, or else."

The visibly nervous men answered with haste, "Yes, ma'am," and returned to their desperate search, palpable tension in the air.

Vrushabh and Sharvari sat petrified, hopeless, at what the strangers were wrecking in that cafe. Vrushabh bent close to Sharvari and whispered desperately, "What are they doing here?

"What do they want?"

Sharvari's voice shook as she replied,

"I'll tell you when we're safe if we make it that far."

Through the storage room door, they could see an evil figure approaching; in his hand was a bright red crowbar. His eyes were black, dead, and cold. His footsteps were the final touch in creating chills down their spines, and, with this, they instinctively clutched each other's hand, too paralyzed by the situation to move a muscle.

The man slowly pushed open the door; the flashlight on his phone lit up the darkness. His eyes skimmed around the room, but he was met by a sudden honk from Sharvari's wheelchair. He spun around, his eyes locking onto Sharvari.

"I found you,"

he growled, his words oozing malice.

But Vrushabh, hidden behind a pile of boxes, sprung into action. With a shot of adrenaline, he grabbed onto the man's foot with a deftly agile motion and impact. His foot met with the crowbar clutched in the man's hand. The weapon writhed through the air like a paper dragon, and Sharvari let out a desperate scream for help, which relented back at the walls of the cafeteria.

The men got a move on towards the storage room. Sharvari heard the creak of the door again and felt a runny chill go down her spine as the other two started to enter. Fear, stale coffee thick in the air. All she could hear was the heavy breathing of the men, the soft rustling. The flash was setting a dim light scattering on the walls, casting eerie shadows in the room. The faces of the men were behind masks, and their eyes were gleaming with malice.

Suddenly, The men lunged at Vrushabh, his fist flying towards his face. Sharvari felt a surge of panic when she saw the punch connect, sending Vrushabh crashing to the floor. The men held Vrushabh down, their hands tightening around his wrists. Sharvari's heart was pounding in her chest as she watched the scene unfold.

His hands had gripped her hair and a sharp, tearing pain was going through her. She tried to scream out, but his hand covered her mouth, muffling the screams. Some droplets of the other man's spittle had fallen on the floor, causing a knot in the pit of her stomach to Sharvari.

As the men shoved them toward the woman, Sharvari noticed her glance with an icy and assessing look. The lady's name was Aarushi.

"I left the parcel in this cafe yesterday," Aarushi said, and her voice was dripping with menace.

"Where is the damn box?" she asked, and her voice was getting louder.

"I don't know," shrugged off Sharvari, and her voice trembled.

"But you threatened my grandmother yesterday," Sharvari said, a cruel smile spreading across Aarushi's face.

Sharvari felt the kick of fear that Aarushi's words sent into her gut. She knew she had to do something to save Vrushabh, but she was helpless against the men's brute strength.

As the men continued to hammer Vrushabh, Sharvari simply felt hopelessly desperate to stop them. "Please, don't hit him," she cried out; however, her words only seemed to turn into air as a part of the lunacy.

She knew she had to act fast to halt the torture. At that very moment, with a heavy breath taken, she said, "OK, I will tell you!" just as the door creaked open and a man in a white shirt with a grey biker mask entered.

The man in the masked t-shirt and white shirt advanced toward the door with the ease of motion, fluid and predatory. The gang of men rushed , yelling at him to leave, but the biker-masked intruder did not move a bit, actually exuding cold tranquillity with his body language and walking farther into the yard.

"Didn't I tell you to leave?" one of the men yelled, with force, while grabbing the masked man by the shoulder.

The intruder jerked his hand off in one motion, speaking from behind the mask, muffled in an inhuman, mechanical voice. "What if I didn't?"

A gloved hand snapped out to close around the man's collar, jerking him closer. In an instant, he threw his fist into the man's face—crunch once, crunch twice—while the sickening crunch of breaking bone echoed through the room and blood sprayed across the white shirt, turning it into a gruesome polka-dot pattern.

The others charged, but at the sight of their companion's face—mangled, pummelled—the horror etched on their features froze them into stillness. The masked man brandished his weapon, next to Vrushabh and Sharvari, who held on to each other, their faces ashen with fear.

"Aarushi! Stop him!" one of the men bellowed, and the woman leapt into action. Her hand pulled out from within the jacket, jerking a pistol out and taking aim. The shot went wide as the intruder kicked the gun from her hand, sending it skittering across the floor. Aarushi jumped for cover, desperately looking around for the weapon.

And at last, he focused on the man, who trained professionally as a fighter and moved with a flow of liquid grace, he sidestepped awkward blows angled at him without a second thought and delivered vicious counter-blows – a man collapsed onto the floor, unconscious, and another screamed with pain as the intruder bent his leg at an awkward angle.

Vrushabh and Sharvari were tied against the wall, holding onto each other so hard as the savage fight continued to storm around them. Then, a masked man walked up toward them, towering over two huddled forms.

"You're safe now," he growled in that disturbing, ever-so-robotic voice.

Aarushi, who had grabbed the gun, pointed at it from behind the intruder. Sharvari "look out!" screamed at the masked intruder. The masked man spun, but not quite quickly enough. The bullet grazed his shoulder, leaving a streak of red. He staggered, then turned his gaze menacingly to Aarushi.

"So, you are Aarushi," he rasped moving toward her. Aarushi's hand trembled violently, and the gun had started shaking. That difficult task was of no pain for the well-trained hands of the intruder; he easily disarmed her, and the pistol fell on the floor with a clatter.

He turned back to them and, in swift moments, unbound his brother and sister. "I stole the parcel from the cafe yesterday," his voice just a little above conversational, and he tied Aarushi with the same ropes, making her hands fast behind her back.

Vrushabh and Sharvari were looking in silent dumbness at what was happening before their eyes and reeling inside their minds from the sudden spurt of violence now taking the place of equitably weird behaviour from the same masked man, who had taken ease with beating their captors and was helping them to escape. Who was he, and what did he want?

He walked towards the door, then turned to look back at them. "Get out of here. Run," he said. Vrushabh took no prompting. He scrambled up on his feet and ran away with Sharvari on his back, not daring to look back.

It was a cool, still day outside with the wail of sirens somewhere in the distance, growing louder and louder as Vrushabh ran with desperate energy, holding Sharvari, their lungs on fire, running at an adrenaline-filled pace. They had escaped the clutches of their abductors, but at what cost?

So he was the masked man who had saved them, yet at the same time, he was a man guilty of shocking brutality. What was on his mind? Were they fully relieved, or was it just the calm before the storm?

As the siren volume increased to an ear-splitting pitch, Vrushabh and Sharvari dodged into an alleyway and doubled over, leaning against the wall, shaking hard with raw fear and relief. It was almost too much to handle. They had survived, but at what cost to their souls?

The next moment, the police arrived, swarming the place. Vrushabh and Sharvari were taken to the station, he took their statements, but their minds were elsewhere, replaying the events in the storage room.

Who was that man in the mask, and why had he let them go? Nothing but questions churned in their heads, and no answer seemed to be easy. All they knew was that this encounter with a mysterious saviour and who he was had changed them forever.

Vrushabh smiled at her warmly and offered, "Maybe, I should drop Sharvari now. It already seems like a long day at the police station.".

"This is not too far; I can walk," she insisted, but he saw the fatigue in her eyes.

He got worried, and hence without making any delay, he requested the officer a wheelchair, which quite surprisingly was seen in no time.

"We have just a few minutes before the sunset- how about a walk down that beautiful corridor ?"

he suggested, and Sharvari was overwhelmed; she agreed.

They strolled, and laughter filled the air after their horrifying day, and then they reached her grand, old villa. Sharvari's grandmother welcomed her with open arms and weeping eyes, and Vrushabh felt a swell of happiness to see her so cherished. With a light heart, he waved goodbye and started walking back home, waiting for the next time he gets to see her without a life-threatening event.

II

The guy from the future

It took Vrushabh some time to compose himself after that ordeal of a day; this was new for him, being the focus in college.

The next morning, he bade his mom and the dog goodbye and left for college. In route, as he passed the closed Cafe-One, he felt a pang. He reached the college gate, where Rohan and Abhay were waiting. Both their faces reflected joy in seeing him.

"How are you?" they asked, bothering their faces with concern.

"Are you hurt? Did they try to abduct you?"

"NO!" Vrushabh responded, shooing away all their concerns. He was very receptive to the idea of diverting their attention by rushing them to class. His friends, playfully resistant, then teasingly submissive, played along. The entrance to the classroom witnessed a sudden silence, with every eye in his class fixated on Vrushabh, magnifying the emotions whirring inside him as they took respective places on their tables. But then, out of nowhere

The whole atmosphere of the class was rendered high with the chit-chat of the students and their laughter. Lost in thought, Vrushabh sat quietly, while the noise in the background mixed with the voice of the professor lecturing. And then, Mr. Kulkarni's footsteps could be heard, after which the classroom went completely silent.

"Everybody, welcome back!" he said,

chirping and beaming a white-and-bright smile. "It has been too long a break, hasn't it? But I am looking forward to diving back into our lessons."

The students' attitude was really good; they showed a spirit of willingness to learn.

Mr Kulkarni took the whiteboard marker, opened it with a pop, and in bold letters, wrote: "Bipolar Junction Transistor."

The entire class seemed to be held up in spontaneous enthusiasm as everybody's heads leaned forward on the seats, except for Vrushabh. He had been distracted by all those remaining whispers and turns of heads by his classmates.

The clear explanation of Mr. Kulkarni and the response of the students made the class active as the class continued. Vrushabh tried his level best to concentrate on the lesson, but his mind went thinking again and again about the mysterious reasons for his classmates' behaviour.

His desire to speak out was yet to commence, and the mobile of Mr. Kulkarni buzzed and an immediate silence wrapped the room. After a little conversation, he stood before Vrushabh with a serious face and said, "The dean wants you at his office right now; it seems important.".

Vrushabh's heartbeat increased as he stood up from his bench. Making decisions in his head about the conversation he might have with the dean, he left the classroom with some anticipation and shaking, following the barely lit corridor. The noise of his steps started to make it feel spooky.

Vrushabh walked to the dean's office with a feeling of apprehension, for he had to be in trouble; something must surely have happened. His mind was still racing with the different possibilities, which only intrigued him. Every step just fanned the fire of curiosity, and now Vrushabh was eager to know more, fill in those blanks that had suddenly cropped up.

Vrushabh made a dour echo blend with its quiet tone. The heavy door screeched open, revealing a figure sitting behind a stack of stuff, whether it was papers or books, he couldn't tell. A figure of authority: the Dean. A stern countenance seemed to cast a shadow in the room. The air was thick with tension, and the faint smell of polished wood and old books amplified the moment.

"Don't you know what the prestige of this college is?" Boomed the Dean's voice,

with a tone of disappointment - the punch of it hits you like a body blow. Every word is purposeful, perioduated to drive a point home with weight. The feeling of dread pooling in his stomach quickened Vrushabh's heart as, finally, the reality of his failure hit him hard. He had become the first student ever to flunk all of the subjects at Newtech Engineering College. His shame and vulnerability lit up like a marquee under the dean's probing gaze.

A tempest was brewing in him—a mixture of shame, fear, and anxiety tore about like a tempest, and it may overflow at any time as he was walking out of the cabin. The hallway felt tight; the walls seemed to close in on him while going back to class as he raced among thoughts of being disappointed in or judged. Other children's laughter struck him from all directions, sharp and scornful and more isolating. Their eyes were on him, their whispers knives each, driving home his failure. He turned away and walked towards the cafeteria—a busy beehive, which was, by the day, becoming more and more alien to him.

Upon their entrance by that time, lunchtime was to keep them enveloped; inside, the cafeteria was thick with smells from frying and freshly baked Chapatis. They sat wedged together at the prolonged tables—a huge racket of laughing and talking. The Contrast was dreadful. Rohan and Abhay beheld him now in the corner, and their faces showed a mingling of anxiety and pluck. The closer they came to him, the more their voices were warm; yet their words were, somehow, very far away, as though spoken through a glass wall. He felt as if he was lost in that maze of thoughts, that the weight of his failure was on his shoulder while all they wanted was to lift his spirits.

At that very moment, Shraddha joined them. She exuded a fierce and playful energy that contrasted with his glumness. She hit his back with playful strength and snapped him out of his reverie. "What was that for?" he yelped, wincing under the bout of sharp pain; it only managed to ground him in a real way. Her laughter—musical and clear—got just barely filtered through; he wrestled with the turmoil in his head.

Yet through this all, he had felt the faint savagery—somehow, just a spark—he could stoke from the flames within him; perhaps he still could make something of himself yet, if only he had the strength to dare. The hours ticked, blended into each other from class to class, and the words of the professors droned as he wrangled alone with himself. And at last, Shraddha and Abhay followed up to date, and the left-over laugh, leaving Rohan with angry Vrushabh. The unspoken words, yet oozing out the tension, their talks bespeak the potential of greatness in friendship.

However, Rohan's concern did not let any of Vrushabh's apathy seep into his voice, which rather rose in urging him to take up his studies seriously. "Vrushabh, you need to stop wasting your potential!" Rohan exclaimed; there was frustration evident in his voice.

"Why do you care so much? It's my life!" Vrushabh shot back, crossing his arms defensively.

"Because I see you throwing it all away! You're stuck in this fog of despair, and I can't just stand by!" Rohan argued, his tone rising.

"Maybe I don't want your help! You think I didn't try, but I tried my level best, but it wasn't enough," Vrushabh shot back with raised anger.

"Then talk to me! Don't just shut me out!" Rohan pleaded, desperation creeping into his voice.

"I want to help you because I want all of us to be together," Rohan said.

Breaking the decade-long fog of despair. The weight at that bus stop was there—ridden with promises that were not delivered, fears unspoken. The bus came for Rohan. As he waved goodbye, Vrushabh felt somewhat grateful and sad. He alone now boarded his bus; the roar of the engine drowned out the world outside.

His heartbeat was still racing as thoughts careened onto the hard challenge ahead, a path to redemption that unwinds like some long, winding road.

Vrushabh sat looking out the window as the bus rambled on. Just then, the phone buzzed. It was a call from his mother. "Your father and I are off to Delhi for an urgent business trip. Food is ready, eat properly, kiddo."

"Oh yes, Mom," shouted Vrushabh in frustration over the device.

By the time the call ended, the battery on his phone was dead. The bus reached his stop, and Vrushabh stepped out from it to find out if he was going to be alone again.

Just as Vrushabh reached his house, he was standing at the door. By this time, though, a weary Vrushabh was not ready to play. He trudged up to his room, flung his bag onto the bed, and then collapsed onto the mattress in all his exhaustion.

Vrushabh jolted awake and turned toward the clock. The night was getting close to midnight when the window in his room's lighting was only a dingy outside light flickering through the window. He gazed towards his home's exterior and noticed a motorcycle standing in the front drive. The rider in front of his biker dismounted and now walked toward the front door. It was the same mask as at the café-one detail. It was at that point that Vrushabh was horrified to see how easily the intruder had opened the door as if it were unlocked.

Jimmy's barking reverberated in the silent house as Vrushabh clutched the cricket bat firmly and crawled down the stairs. The man with the mask was sitting comfortably on the couch with Jimmy, caressing him as if he were a friend. Vrushabh carried up the bat and was about to hit the intruder when suddenly Jimmy barked, cautioning the man. Within the twinkling of an eye, he had caught hold of the bat with one hand, leaving Vrushabh imbalanced and dumbfounded.

The lights flickered back to life, and Vrushabh was staring face-to-face with the masked man. Befitting, he began to remove his helmet, and Vrushabh was met with features that were hauntingly too familiar. Vrushabh then found himself struggling to place the features—some sort of deja vu washed over him.

"What do you want?"

Vrushabh asked, trying to still the tremble in his voice.

"How did you get in?"

He chuckled again, this time coming across as forlorn, and whispered,

"Was I always this clueless?" Holding a glass of water, he walked into the room from the kitchen and gave it to Vrushabh.

"How did I get in? Why does Jimmy like me? Why do I know my way in the kitchen?"

He stops yet again, his eyes glistening with hope. "Don't you get it?"

Vrushabh shook his head. What? What am I supposed to do?

The man hunched forward and frowned. "Guess."

Vrushabh's mind was galloping with the jigsaw pieces of the puzzle to line up. "Are you? a gangster? Here for the money?"

Very angrily, the man sighed.

"I'm you, you moron!" he said.

"From the future. I have come to help you change the course of history leading to the end of the world."

Vrushabh continued to stare at Steven, his mouth open.

"The future? This man speaks about the falling and destruction of the world."

Gaping at Jimmy, he shook his head in disbelief. "This can't be real."

Yes, the future Vrushabh nodded gravely.

"It's true. The choices you are going to make are going to have devastating consequences. You have to trust me and let me help you."

Vrushabh fell silent, his mind whirling with the bombshell.

"But.. I have my studies and friends. I just can't get up and leave everything."

"Your degree wouldn't save a thing if there is no future," said the future Vrushabh. "Believe me, Vrushabh. I've seen what's incoming, and it's not very. We need to act."

Vrushabh was unimpressed, though. The loyalties to his present life overrode any dire warnings from his future self. "I'm sorry but I can't help you. I have to focus on my path." Vrushabh felt that his future self was hiding something from him.

Vrushabh, his eyes full of disappointment for the future that lay ahead, took a deep breath. He slipped his hand in the pocket and pulled out a note. He inscribed a telephone number on it and said, "Change your mind, call on this number. I would be waiting." He threw it away on the table. While carrying the mask in his hand, he turned back to walk toward the door.

As the noise of the motorcycle ebbed away into the darkness of night, finally, he was left with just the note. Vrushabh felt a sinking feeling inside him. Had he done the right thing? What if his future self were telling the truth? Vrushabh felt as though the weight of the world rested on his shoulders, and he knew this important decision he was going to make would shape not just his future but the fate of the whole planet. The next day happened to be a Wednesday morning, bright and breezy. Vrushabh opted for a leisurely walk, for his spirits needed some cheering up.

It was a usual Wednesday afternoon, and of course, destiny brought him to his favourite place for the umpteenth time that fateful morning: Cafe-One, where he found Sharvari once again, lazing in that wheelchair, as usual, just in front of the entrance. A genuinely huge smile lit up his face, and he went, in a very excited tone, "Hey!" Sharvari gave the same back with so much rad that she could only manage to say something cheesy like, "Long time no see!" "So, what brings you here on this beautiful day?" inquired Vrushabh.

"Oh, you know, just missing my work at the café," sighed a wistful Sharvari. "What we do makes our being, right?" Vrushabh commented, at which he received a nod from Sharvari.

Vrushabh asked "what is that you were going to tell that day in the cafe?" But distracting Vrushabh that look dawned in Sharvari's eyes with all the opportunist ideas: "Say, how about we get some breakfast now?" "A classic can never be said no to. That, come on," said Vrushabh with all eyes open towards this opportunity.

Sizzling dosas filled the air as they sat huddled in one of those little cosy restaurants. He was an utter gentleman and relished every morsel. It was on this occasion, with a lifetime ambition to become a celebrated physicist, that Sharvari found an opportunity to pour her heart out, and Vrushabh was busy imbibing the words along with the dosa.

"Well, you know, this whole time dilation thing has fascinated me since I was a little kid," she said, her eyes twinkling. "So many ways to travel through time! Isn't that just blowing your mind?"

Vrushabh listened with a swelling heart, appreciating at once the enthusiasm of the stranger. That is until Sharvari said something that broke his heart: that she has Amyotrophic Lateral Sclerosis. Vrushabh felt as though he was struck by a bolt of electricity as soon as he had the thought that she might not live to fulfil her aspirations for this paralysing disease.

"But you know what? I've taken my destiny and decided to make the most of it, given all circumstances. My café, my family— it's my world now."

Vrushabh felt something strong inside him: a lot of pity and a craving to be part of the change. "I don't want you to give up, Sharvari," he said with a choking voice.

"No, I won't," she said, looking straight back at him.

There was an impulsive urge and thought so raucous: the time had come for them to say their goodbyes.

He wanted to do something, do anything that marked the difference in life for Sharvari. He ran home, his eyes catching the paper lying everywhere with a note promising him all success and making it big. But he did not wait for a better moment, just picked up the phone and waited. The connection was made, and he heard a familiar voice. "One condition: I will help you. Meet me at the park near your house, and we will talk," the Future Self answered, a hint of amusement creeping into his voice.

Vrushabh ran eagerly to the park, his heart pounding in excitement. As he approached his future he was about to blurt out his question. "If I help you, I want the cure for Sharvari's ailment in the future, and the test papers for my supplementary exam. Do we have a deal?"

To his surprise, his future self burst into laughter.

"You know, never in my life did I ever think my younger self would long for that," he chuckled, shaking his head. "But I'll tell you what—I can provide the cure and the test papers, and in return, I need you to do one thing for me."

Think in his mind he won't be able to prove because his timeline is dead, and he just lied to his younger self. Vrushabh leaned in, his curiosity piqued.

"Your first job is to make Sharvari your girlfriend, or at least get close to her," said his future self with a grin growing on his face, mischievous.

"What?!" Vrushabh just could not believe his ears, for just now his voice had gone several decibels higher than it would under normal circumstances. Was this both a game and a joke from the universe, perceived by his future self?

Future Him then winked and smiled, saying, "Wink and you will get it, all in one go, right at the end." Romeo, you're on!

"Vrushabh could only look on in amazement as his Future Self melted into the crowd, leaving him with a head full of questions and a heart full of fresh determination to help Sharvari and unravel the mysteries of his future.".

He then went on to explain to Vrushabh the situation at hand and said that he needed another time machine so that he could go back to his timeline when things were put right. He had one, he said but stressed that to move between the two timelines, a second machine had to be placed into the time stream.

"They're coming to stop us with the time they've stolen," he warned.

"Who are they?" Vrushabh pressed.

"Patience, we'll reveal their identity in good time," said the future Vrushabh, therefore smothering truth in mystery and uncertainty—thickening the air with tension and intrigue.

III

Kakbhushundi's pond

It was a new morning, about 6:30 AM when the golden rays of the sun began to pass through Sharvari's room curtains. Slowly, she got up from the peaceful sleep, feeling something naggingly tired as if she had not at all rested. Her cluttered desk, beside the bed, carried the weight of unique formulations and equations regarding time dilation, remnants of her late-night musings.

Just as she washed up, her grandmother's voice echoed, calling her to come and have breakfast. The smell of dabeli and shrikhand wafted through the air and drove out all of her sleepiness.

"Hurry up, finish your breakfast! I have an event to go to this morning," urged the grandmother in a slightly husky but urgent voice.

"Okay," said Sharvari, taking a big bite of the dabeli and enjoying the spicy taste.

"What's that you're always scribbling in your notebook?" her grandmother asked, curiosity lighting up her eyes.

"Nothing much," Sharvari hesitated, a hint of shyness creeping into her tone.

"Finish up; you have an event to get ready for," reminded her grandmother and playfully teased.

"Okay, don't tell me then," Sharvari shot back, a smirk playing on her lips.

After breakfast, her grandmother pushed her wheelchair into the drawing room and switched on the TV, running her favourite movie, "Ramayana: The Legend of Prince Ram." However, the movie did not interest Sharvari, and she turned it off to take her phone and start scrolling through social media.

A little while passed until her grandmother came in, smartly attired in a green sari that shimmered under the rays of the morning sun.

"How do I look?" she asked, pirouetting gently.

"Young as ever," said Sharvari with a rakish smirk.

Her grandmother instructed the servant to follow Sharvari as she began preparing to leave. Just then, Sharvari's phone beeped. It was a direct message from Vrushabh: "Hey. My friends and I are going to take a tour of the temple just at the edge of town. Want to go with me?

She felt her heartbeat for this was the very first time that someone would be inviting her to join in on something like this. Sharvari wheeled herself up to her granny to ask permission for the trip.

"No, that's it," replied her granny, sharp enough to leave no room for negotiation.

"But I want to go!" protested Sharvari.

"You better listen to me," warned her granny, her eyes widening with an authoritative stance.

Sharvari's face fell at the news of her grandmother being away. "Nina, a cup of coffee!" she ordered with a tinge of frustration in her tone.

"Just a moment," Nina said and left the room.

Sharvari took the phone and called up Vrushabh. "I'm ready for the trip," she said, her bubbling voice filled with excitement.

"Great! I shall be there at your house in 30 minutes!" Vrushabh responded excitedly.

She dressed in a hurry; her heart was racing with excitement. As Nina came with her coffee, she slipped out of the villa unnoticed by any person and waited by the gate. Minutes ticked like hours as she saw cars whizz by; her excitement was tinged with anxiety.

A 9-seater finally arrived, from which Vrushabh alighted, helped her into the vehicle, and put away her wheelchair in the trunk. Just as they were about to drive off, Nina stood before them.

"Sharvari, come out of the car!" she ordered.

"Just this once, please! It's my first time out with friends!" Sharvari told her, her eyes wide and innocent.

"But I have orders not to let you go," Nina insisted.

Just as Sharvari's hope began to fade, Vrushabh intervened. "Please, just help us this once, Miss Nina," he said with a charming smile.

Nina, torn between duty and the pleading eyes of the young girl, looked on hesitantly. "What would I tell your grandmother?" she asked.

"We'll be back before sunset, I promise," Vrushabh assured her. "And Sharvari's grandmother will be back by night."

Turning reluctantly, she sighed. "All right, but don't forget your promise," Nina threatened as she walked back to the villa.

Free at last, Sharvari felt the exhilaration of relief. Vrushabh showed her his friends: Rohan, Abhay, Sharadha, Devshri, and their guide, Rohan's elder brother Mitesh.

"Hello, all!" Sharvari greeted them; her face brightened with a beaming smile. Then, her curiosity drew her attention to a figure standing back there in a mask. "Who's he?"

"That's my cousin Mohit. He doesn't like to talk much," Vrushabh explained.

He cranked up the music as they hit the highway, filling the car with lots of vibrant rhythms and beats.

They laughed and sang along, their voices with the sound of the engine as they moved through the city into the lush green nature.

The car came to a sudden halt, spewing smoke from the bonnet. Mitesh looked flummoxed, for he did not know what to do with the car in that remote area, without a garage in sight.

"Does anyone here know how to fix a car?" he inquired from all those around.

Abhay and Vrushabh exchanged glances, then turned towards Rohan. "Fine, I know how," Rohan said confidently.

Relieved, they all stared out the window as Rohan got out and began tinkering around the engine, his hands moving deftly as if he were some sort of master craftsman shaping his piece of perfection.

Moments of tension later, Rohan returned to the car, his face reddened. "I fixed it," he confessed sheepishly, "but the battery is dead.".

"Leave it to me," Abhay said and jumped out of the vehicle. He went behind the car and told Mitesh to start it while he pushed.

"How can you do that all alone?" Mitesh asked with surprise.

"I'll push too," Vrushabh added, going to the rear of the car. Both of them started pushing with all their strength as the car began to move a little.

With a grunt, Mitesh turned the key, and the engine came to life. The boys leapt backwards as they exploded into laughter in celebration of their small victory.

"Let's keep going!" Sharvari cheered, her spirits lifted.

The journey further became the essence of his laughter and music, sewing the tapestry of friendship and adventure Sharvari was looking for. This trip was not going to be an escape; rather, it was a step into a world where one feels alive, cherished, and free.

Finally, the group began the thrilling journey. Their hearts were filled with excitement and a sense of eagerness. Mithesh's car came to a slow stop at the foot of the mountain. The friends stepped out of the car, smelling the fresh, unpoisoned air. Abhay and Sharadha held each other real tight, taking pictures excitedly about the towering peak that lay ahead.

Devshri, being the nice girl, helped Sharvari out of the car and onto her wheelchair. Her eyes widened with amazement, and she quipped, "I can't track, you know." But Mithesh, beaming with a reassuring smile, revealed their plan, "We know there's a straight way to go at the top where we can use the wheelchair."

The joy was writ large on Sharvari's face as Vrushabh rushed to her rescue and took her wheelchair, leading her along the path. Rohan, the diligent one, picked up the bags, while Mithesh parked the car. With great spirits, they began to climb higher into the mountain while Mohit disappeared on his own path.

They started to climb, and soon Rohan and Mithesh joined them. Their laughter and chatter echoed as they went higher. Sharvari expressed her feeling, not because of the temple but due to the memories that she would gather with her friends. Devshri, mischievously expressive, turned around and said, "Just reserve your words till you see the temple."

She is a person of science," Vrushabh chimed in, the habitual Sharvari defender. Sharvari turned toward him, a grateful smile playing on her lips, her heart fluttering with the warmth of his support.

Abhay, the everlasting joker, jumped in with "Then Rohan is the guy for you then," and mischievously winked at Rohan. The argument went on, but Vrushabh felt his mind wandering off as he desperately thought of some idea to impress Sharvari. As he looked at her, the words caught in his throat, and he could feel the heat flushing up to his cheeks.

Sharvari touched his hand suddenly, her touch like a shiver down the spine. "Everybody's getting ahead," she said, soft and melodious. "So that's it," he replied, his voice trembling with nervousness. He quickened up his pace, determined to catch up with the rest of the group.

While they were about to reach the top of the mountain, right before them emerged the ancient temple of Mahadeva, whose stone walls gleamed with the rays of the sun. This more-than-2,000-year-old temple would soothe the nerves of whoever took its glimpse. The breathtaking view of the town at the foot of the temple and by its sides, along with winds whispering secrets from heaven as it seemed, was there. They reached the entranceway to the temple.

Intricate carvings on the temple walls drew their attention to the figures, each telling a story of its own. There at the door stood a priest, clad in saffron robes with a long smooth head full of overgrown hairs. Taking their shoes off at the threshold, they went inside the temple where dry air and palpable energy that seemed to vibrate through the stone filled their senses.

They prayed to Mahadeva, and Sharvari, ever the curious one, asked the priest about the history of the temple. "How was the temple built?" she inquired, her voice laced with wonder. With a warm smile, he began to weave a story of Kakbhushundi, an ardent devotee of Mahadeva.

The story was much like the unfurling of tapestry, wherein every thread is intricately woven into the very fabric of devotion and destiny. Kakbhushundi, a stern devotee, once diverted the attention of Mahadeva and failed master by not recognizing Shri Hari or Vishnu Dev. For this mischief, he was put under a curse by Mahadev to take birth as a snake for one thousand rebirths. But under the compelling miserable condition of his master, Mahadeva further modified the curse that after his one thousand rebirth as a snake, he would take birth as Brahma and be a devotee of Ram.

But fate had other plans, and Kakbhushundi made the same error again—disrespecting the great sage who, in anger, cursed Kakbhushundi to rebirth as a crow. But naturally, the crow form was peculiarly significant for Kakbhushundi because it was the form of his most endearing Prince Ram. Kakbhushundi longed to find out and understand much more about these avatars of Vishnu after his death. Due to his devotion, he is granted a power that gives him the ability to move as one desires through time, hence seeing the Ramayana eleven times and the

Mahabharata sixteen times.

It is said that the temple was built by Kakbhushundi himself, while at the back was a pond which brought about time travel. Near the pond stood an ancient stone statue of a humanoid figure with a crow's head, explaining the unique form of Kakbhushundi.

Everybody listened to the tale, enthralled, except for Sharvari and Rohan. As they emerged from the temple, Sharvari launched into a long diatribe about the loopholes in the theory of relativity, how travel through time for Kakbhushundi was impossible. Rohan, the man of science, nodded vigorously in assent with her, full of conviction in his voice.

Devshri was undaunted by their incredulity and asserted, "Whatever you say, I believe in the tale that the priest told us," and the others in the group chimed in agreement. Vrushabh, ever playing the pacifist, suggested, "Let's not fight, guys. Why don't we go see the pond?"

As the group walked towards the pond, they were all taken by its beauty. The clear water sparkled in the sunlight's lances, while in separate shoals agile fish flickered lightly with the game. On all sides of the pond, there was greenery, swayed by a weak wind, with the air filled with the sweet smell of wildflowers.

That image of the crow, beside the pond, was an epitome of craftsmanship. It emulated every element of Kakbhushundi's story. Cold winds touched the face, and above, in a mesmerising dance, crows flew.

Shraddha, the photographer, wanted to click a group picture and so asked everybody to gather around her. "I want to be the star today," she said with a glint in her eye. Devshri, ever the joker, quipped back, "But I want to be a star," her laughter peeling like music.

Shraddha nodded with a smile on her face. "Next time maybe," she said, and her eyes sparkled. Then Devshri, elated by the happy thought, enquired that Sharvari be included in the centre in the group photo. "She is the new member of our squad," said Devshri in her warm and welcoming voice.

Shraddha, after a little hesitation, agreed. She then turned towards Abhay, her voice sharp, her eyes anger-filled, "I want also a picture with you later." Abhay, his eyes moist with emotion, replied softly, "As you say, boss."

The group lined up for the picture, and Mithesh snapped the shot. Later, as they dispersed, Vrushabh felt himself drawn towards the pond again. He knelt beside the pool, his fingers tracing its smooth water surface. Much to his surprise, it didn't seem that deep at all for a pond. Rohan raised an eyebrow in curiosity, observing, "It's really weird that there's no kind of algae growing inside a well this big." Vrushabh agreed with Rohan's analysis, too; his mind was working on various possibilities, convinced this was no ordinary pond.

Devshri's tour of the ancient Temple came to an abrupt end. She unscrewed her water bottle, only to find it almost empty, just one single drop trickling down her throat. Thirst clawed at her throat, and she spun around to face Vrushabh, who was busy adjusting Sharvari's wheelchair, his eyes bright with excitement. "The water there is so reflective; we should take a pic!" he exclaimed, pointing at the shimmering pond.

"Do you have water?" Desperation was creeping into the voice of Devshri. Vrushabh shook his head. The young girl looked around the group; her heart sank. Abhay and Shraddha were lost in their world, as laughter was found echoing between the two, Rohan was standing pretty far away to be of any help, and, lastly, Mitesh was looking with a mischievous grin. "Do you have water by any chance?" she asked with hope in her heart.

Mitesh replied with a grin, "Yes, I have some!"

"Then give it to me!" Devshri urged her voice with a mix of urgency and humour written on her face.

He instead turned and dashed off, a gurgle of laughter bubbling out of him. He ran, his foot hit a stone, and he tumbled toward Sharvari's wheelchair. In less than half a second, something in Vrushabh leapt forward; some part of his instincts kicked in, and he dived to catch Sharvari as she started to fall.

"Whoa!" others gasped, their hearts racing at this sudden action. Vrushabh thudded on the ground with a grimace—sharp pain shot through his back.

"Are you okay?" Rohan and Mitesh reached to help get him to his feet, concerned.

"My back!" he yelled, half in laughter, half wincing.

"Oh, thank God you're okay!" Sharvari broke into giggles, lightening the mood with hers as she nestled down into her wheelchair.

Devshri and Mitesh exchanged some guilty looks, their faces trickling with apologies.

"Sorry, we didn't mean it to be like this," Devshri ducked in a now-softened voice.

"Don't worry, guys, I'm okay," he added consolingly though still otherwise would he look, continuing groaning in pain.

As the tension broke, all of them agreed to call it a day and proceeded for lunch at a high-end restaurant. Rohan took over the responsibility of Sharvari's wheelchair and began moving her through the rocky mountain carefully.

Mohit rejoined the crew at the base of the mountain and his presence instantly uplifted the mood. He pulled Vrushabh to a corner where both could talk without being overheard. From a distance, Rohan watched the two of them: they almost looked like brothers, sharing the resemblance so closely.

After a short chat, all got integrated again into the group when Devshri asked about a restaurant that was on the other side with a wild jungle theme. All got more or less convinced, and excitement was running through the group.

Mitesh took the keys and headed toward the car. The car sputtered but failed to catch fire. "Abhay, give a hand please?" he said; there was some frustration in his voice.

With a push from Abhay, the car roared to life, and they all piled in. Laughter and chatter fill the air as they drive toward the Rainforest Zone, the town's most famous jungle-themed restaurant.

The music was on, the wind blowing through their hair, and they sang along to it while the atmosphere remained light with merriment. All of a sudden, a sharp cry pierced the joy. "Ahh!" Mohit exclaimed, clutching his arm in pain.

"Stop the car!" he shouted, his voice rising with panic.

"We're almost there!" Mitesh begged, his foot pressing harder on the accelerator.

The car came to a screeching halt at the entrance of the restaurant, and they all scrambled out with concern written all over their faces as they circled Mohit. "What's wrong?" they asked in unison.

"Nothing, I'm okay," he said, but his voice shook a bit. Vrushabh observed something awkward; as Mohit kept talking, his hand picturedly appeared to shatter completely into a weird-looking structure of cubes of light.

He abruptly hid his hand behind the pure, white gloves, his face trying hard to smile in nervousness, "Aren't you all hungry? Let's get inside, come."

They both had to agree to get inside the restaurant after much persuasion from Vrushabh that Mohit would be fine. The ambience was a beautiful one with lots of greenery and the sounds of animals somewhere at a distance. Rabbits hopped around and frolicked, with peacocks strutting in cages, adding to the quirkiness of the place.

When you stepped inside, the place was wonderfully decorated in the most exotic manner, with marble floors and shining wooden tables, and surrounded by soft comfy sofas. The smell of some delicious food wafted and stimulated their already growling tummy so much more.

As they seated themselves, Shraddha rang the bell, and in a few seconds, the attendant approached their table. They ordered Paneer Angara for all and Butter Naan, then chapatis for Devshri.

Between all the banter and laughter, Shraddha leaned a little towards Vrushabh. "Why don't you invite her to our college's annual fest?" she said, with an evident teasing gleam in her eyes.

"I thought I would study for my exam," he replied, a little embarrassed in his voice.

"Rohan will guide you on that! You should pay a visit to Sharvari," sharing this idea, he nudged Rohan. "I think that would be superb! Bring Mohit along as well."

"Okay, I will try," Vrushabh surrenderedr to the warmth of belonging.

And then the dishes arrived, and each was so pungent that it was impossible not to make the eyes open so wide with relish to view the food. Lunch was almost enchanting in its ambience; the people leaned forward eagerly and joined with rejoicing all over as they feasted.

It wasn't long before the meal became a festival, with every subsequent bite enjoying flavours that pirouetted across his taste buds, the stories that flowed out matching the music that gently wafted through the restaurant. They joked and ribbed each other about foibles of the day, and soon all the laughter caught, lifting through the dining room.

In all the confusion and joy, Vrushabh looked up at Mohit and they exchanged glances. There was a kind of silent understanding between them. "You haven't got things even an inch closer to our mission, have you?" Mohit whispered, though his tone was something between serious and playful.

"I really am trying my best, but she just..." Vrushabh trailed as the blush spread on his cheeks at the thought of Sharvari.

"See you haven't understood. We don't have time, bud. They are coming closer," Mohit insisted, urgency creeping into his voice.

"Let me try once more, just see," Vrushabh promised Mohit, an almost light of resolution tentatively catching his eyes.

The rest of the meal continued companionably, warm with laughter, chaff, and just a hint of secrets. They were friends—that tight bunch you see the world over—not separated by experience, laughter, and the secrets that hung in the air, unspoken, waiting to be unravelled one by one.

As they came out from the restaurant, an unnerving feeling began; a black muscle car loomed right behind them, like a shadow. Feeling that kind of energy, Mithesh braked their 9-seater all of a sudden. The group was held by fear as Sharvari clutched Shraddha and Deavshir's hands together—both heartbeats racing. Mithesh gunned the engine, trying to get away; it surged ahead to block their path. With mixed feelings of curiosity and dread, Abhay stepped out to be met by a figure in black who had emerged from the vehicle, much like a spectre out of the car in mystery and menace.

IV

A road side incident

The car screeched to a stop and his heart thumped inside his chest—a savage drumbeat of fear and adrenaline. He flung the door open and got out, to be met by the chilling sight of Arushi, clad in a sleek black suit that seemed to absorb the fading light. Her face, so familiar from the cafe-one incident, over an unnerving transformation for her age, seemed like she aged 10 years just in a few weeks.

"Why are you following us?" he demanded, his voice quaking with anger mixed with dread.

Arushi produced a gun, which almost shone as she grabbed it firmly in a threatening gesture. "Out!" she mumbled - cold like ice and very cutting. It seemed to pass through the air, already heavy with tension. Racing, hearts making speedway for air, they settled on the punishing cold ground with hands clasped behind their heads in full view of their vulnerability.

And, of course, Mohit - the last to leave - tarried with a mask between him and the unfolding nightmare

.

"Get it off me!" Arushi snarled anger etched into her voice.

Scrabbling with a racing heart, he pulled off the mask, but in that moment a jagged stone of his yard flashed for Vrushabh from behind Mitesh. He flung it at her with a quick, desperate motion.

She ducked, reflexes sharpened by experience, but in that fleck of a second, Abhay slipped from her hold. "You little..."

she snarled as her eyes narrowed and the gun swivelled towards Vrushabh. Mohit launched himself at her, but Arushi counterbalanced with a brutal kick that sent him sprawling backwards, the wind knocked out of his lungs.

"You should have passed me the parcel while you had a chance,"

she jeered, her confidence shining like a dark aura. Bloodied, Mohit pulled himself up to launch a punch that she blocked easily and then jabbed a counterattack that sent blood from his nose streaming down his face. "Not so intimidating now, are you?" she mocked, but with all his blood racing, Mohit growled, "I've only just started."

He charged again, fueled by a mix of rage and fear, but Arushi caught his fist, striking his forehead with a brutal blow that left him reeling. "What's happened to her?" Vrushabh asked, perplexed at this transformation in their once-familiar friend. "How the hell should I know?" Mohit retorted, struggling to keep pace with her relentless assault.

They both pounced forward with one unified movement, but even as Abhay and Vrushabh charged, Arushi had Vrushabh sent crashing to the ground with a swift kick, while Abhay's attack met a punishing headbutt that left Abhay gasping on the ground, stars dancing in his vision. Hell broke loose, a whirlwind of violence and desperation.

In the melee, he vanished from her sight and reappeared behind her like a ghost.

He kicked her hard and she lost balance. The success was for a moment because things were turning worse. Rohan took the opportunity and ran towards the fallen gun. "Toss it to me!" Mohit shouted, feeling surge of adrenaline. Rohan gasped, and he fell to his knees, but the gun did not go off; it slipped from Mohit's hand, and its bullet got scratched on forehand of Vrushabh, there, leaving painful marks, something like a mark that would later appear completely healed on Mohit's forehand and very old by then.

The battle escalated to new heights as Mohit responded with a storm of kicks, but Arushi counted on her part, sending her punches down like thunderclaps, each resonant sound ringing with a jarring finality.

"A timeline hopper, such as you, will never stop us,"

she sneered, revealing that she knew about time machines. Bloodied but unbowed, Mohit replied, "Tell me something I don't know.

In the middle of their struggle, Arushi yanked off his gloves so she could expose his disintegrating hand, shimmering with otherworldly light.

"Another timeline corrupter,"

she said happily as the smile grew sinister, realising the anomaly that he could represent. The air hung heavy with the revelation—a bad promise of what was to come.

At that moment, from the side, Shraddha appeared and threw a branch towards Arushi, like a bat, but agilely, she jumped off the track. The moment had come for Mohit: he banged the back of her head with something that looked like a solid blow and pushed her into unconsciousness. He donned his gloves rapidly, anxious to obscure what lurked within him from eager eyes.

The group gathered, tending to their wounds as the adrenaline started to subside. Shraddha and Devashri bandaged Vrushabh's injury, their hands shaking with residual fear. Rohan helped Sharvari, still shaken, her eyes wide with the remnants of terror. Mitesh tried to lighten the mood with

"Are you guys okay?"

The collective groan of "What does it look like?" flushed him with embarrassment as the weight of their situation pressed down on them.

Frustrated, he turned on the ignition; the car coughed in protest. He banged the steering wheel in irritation, creating a rather rude row in the process, and everyone winced at the temper that seemed to flare and settle in realisation. Abhay was determined, so he moved to the front and began to push, while Mitesh turned on the ignition again. The engine roared to life, and relief swept over them.

As they sped off, the sky fired with colours of orange against the tussle they had just been through. Easy drove the car into the villa—Sharvari's grandmother. Flanking at the gate, she was with crossed arms and a fiery expression painted on her face. Sharvari feared, for she jerked backwards against getting out of the car, for the weight of their encounter rested heavily on her shoulders.

"It's okay,"

Vrushabh said, his voice wavering.

"Under the worst scenario, she will just scold you."

Sharvari took a deep breath to face her grandmother. Shraddha helped her into her wheelchair as the stern voice of her grandmother cut the air. "Didn't I tell you not to go?"

"I don't listen to anything!"

Sharvari retorted, desperate, lacing her voice as she fought against the tide of authority. "Say goodbye to your friends. We'll talk later," her grandmother ordered, ushering her inside with an iron grip.

"Dadiji(grandmother), sunn o!(Listen)"

Sharvari implored, but her grandmother proved inexorable, so she had to go back to her room. A sulking Sharvari did so, watching the friends departing in the vehicle and already feeling the ghost of their collective experience hanging heavy in the air.

Night fell around them, and neither friend said a word, each lost in thought, the adrenaline of the encounter still coursing through them. They had faced danger together, forming bonds in the heat of conflict, but there were large emotional scars, and with Arushi's motives remaining a mystery—all else clear, their adventures surely didn't end here. On the horizon now flickered uncertainty; danger never being too far behind in their world.

V

The Time machine

As Vrushabh and Mohit get back from the trip, Vrushabh calls Mohit his future self.

"What do we do next ?" With a low voice "You haven't done anything" "you failed the trip to the Temple"

Explaining to him that that was their best opportunity.

Vrushabh expresses "Where were you when we went to the temple" in a screeching voice

"I .." "I went to look at the time machine," he pleaded.

Hearing about the time machine, Vrushabh forgot all his questions and asked future Vrushabh,

"Can I see the Time machine ?" he requested.

The future self refused the question altogether. With promise in his eyes and a cute, innocent smile, he again asked,

"Vrushabh, please". Seeing his younger self smiling he agrees to show him the time machine. Future Vrushabh picks up his bike and tells Vrushabh to sit back. As they drive in the night through the city lights. Future Vrushabh asked, "What if you don't like the person you become?"

while slowing down his bike.

Vrushabh replied,

"As mom said, no matter where you end up, you will always be a hero to us", with a slightly soft voice.

Future Vrushabh picks up the speed and then takes the same road to the temple. And stopped near the foot of the mountain again. As the Future self turned on a flashlight which faded away the darkness, he was able to see nothing,g, and with disappointment in his eyes, he looked at his future,e lf, who rep, lied, "Wait just a se " and", And pulled out some kind of key which was glowing neon blue and was like a box in shape.

He put that key on the ground, and, in just a few sec, a circular portal-like door images from ground as It was stored in the fourth dimension plane, which could store anything and everything as long as it's made up of matter and its a common site in the near future. With a marvellous look, it was the time. Though it looked like a door, it was responsible for making travel through time and timeline possible, which was given by their friend.

The time machine door had a neon light glowing in it. And in the centre, the light was the most dense. Future Vrushabh explains that the Time machine that they have from his timeline can't be used to travel back to the timeline without a time machine from this timeline.

After the explanation confused Vrushabh asked "Why did you hide it out here, near the temple"

This place had the most efficient energy particles that allowed the smooth conversation of practice to form light particles, which in the end, then converted for the traveller to successfully travel through time.

This place had a longitudinal environment suitable for travel in time as the practicals are mostly stable when the time machine is near the temple area. Young Vrushabh further asked,

"Then can it be due to the time travelling pound at the top of the mountain?" "That the particles become stable for time travel",

Future Vrushabh" I don't think so", with slight thought-provoking his mind.

The Kakbhushundi legend doesn't go hand in hand with the modern theory of time travel. The theory was given by somehow knowing the legend as to why the particles are mostly stable near the mountain is not clear.

"Now that you have seen the time machine, what do you think you would take your job more seriously?"

Future Vrushabh asked with a motivational tone "Yes, we'll try my best I will say my timeline", young Vrushabh replied.

As they were young, Vrushabh asked,

"Do you think there can be any other way to time travel?".

" Yes" In the future, Vrushabh began storing the time machine in the fourth dimension key. They decide to leave the palace, and on their way back home, they stop at a local street vendor to enjoy some street food.

Where Vrushabh orders two plates of bhel stating that they are the best in the town. Future Vrushabh refers to enjoying it while you can. It won't be there in the future and he misses the treaty food from when he was his age.

As they were having this conversation Vrushabh expressed to his future self that he thought that I would love to be someone like him. I think it would be much stronger, with great bulk and a time machine to top all that.

Listening to this, his response was,

"I never managed to save anything special to me, never in my life did things that I should have done; in other words, my life was nothing but a worthless one". Young Vrushabh,

"Don't say stupid things like that," with a strong voice.

As discussed, you travelled here to correct your mistake, so don't be disappointed with what his future version has done. We have to work it out and they just have to make everything correct again.

As the Behl arrived at their table a familiar face entered the same place for some snakes. It was Abhy who was surprised to see both of them there and asked,

"Are they brothers or just cousins?"

He referred to the future Vrushabh as Mohit. He sat along with them and began asking Vrushabh what his plan for the annual fest was. Everyone was going to be there, and that silly Rohan had suggested a drama of the legend of Kakbhushundi.

He was put as the head writer for the drama department. Vrushabh replied "Isn't it quite that he isn't writing a sci-fi"

"Yeah I know"

Abhy responded. Abhy expressed that Vrushabh should ask Sharvari to be in the annual fest as thinks they would be a great pair. The Future Vrushabh

"Yes, you're correct, and I will convince him to be at the annual fest", and they both take their leave and disappear in the city lights.

The young Vrushabh turned on the TV, with the empty house echoing only with the sound of footsteps.

"If you're someone from the future, which stocks should I invest in?" The eyes of the young man sparkled with hope. His older version smiled. It was a bittersweet laugh that cloaked the amount of regret inside.

"Kid, you forgot what we have to do first,"

he said, revealing the ghost of his past mistakes. He spoke of how he had blown money on things that would bring momentary pleasure, wanting to spend all their parents' money. The weight hung heavily in the air, reminding him of lost chances and unfulfilled dreams.

Diffidently, he disclosed,

"She is our wife," a secret stored within the dark recesses of his heart, wherein love and longing were an inseparable blend with heady excitement and irresponsible ambition. This was like a bolt of lightning to young Vrushabh, and what erupted was a crossfire of emotions: joy, sorrow, and confusion. The mention of their wife Sharvari warmed his heart, and the weight of mistakes that they had made weighed heavily upon him.

Behind them stood a timekeeping commission; ahead of them loomed a spectre of all their failures. Their future self lay down, weakened by infection from time travel; the future had grim portents. He was dying, and the urgency of their situation pressed down on them like a heavy shroud. "I don't know the cure," he let out, his voice trembling with pain and vulnerability. Each word was a dagger, piercing through the fabric of their hopes.

Standing at the cusp of changing historical events, the future self wanted fast action from young Vrushabh. "Invite Sharvari to the annual fest," he urged, his desperation tingling into his voice. "You need to impress her; we're running out of time." The flicker of hope that had ignited in Vrushabh again got cloaked by the fear of failure.

He remembered Arushi: that unpredictable force from the past. In her presence, future Vrushabh knew, things seemed always to get complicated.

"She might be there in the commission,"

the narrow eyes of the future Vrushabh looked concerned. His mind was filled with dread that Arushi might be somewhere in the shadows to remind him that his entire road ahead was full of dangers.

Vrushabh, determined, picked up his phone. His heart raced at an accelerating rate, and he dialled Sharvari's number. Anticipation swirled in him like a gale. "Will you come to the college fest with me?"

he asked, his voice hardly concealing the excitement and anxiety running down his veins.

"Yes, but Rohan had already asked me, so may he come along?"

Her words broke his hopes into a million pieces like a thunderbolt. He felt the first ripple of shock, and "What!!!" was the only reply that wrenched its way out from his lips. His mind got muddled, and he couldn't respond to her words. Rohan? When was that?

He agreed to the arrangement, even though a storm was brewing inside him. A feeling of disappointment and determination swirled together in his chest. He hung up the call. Uncertainty pressed down on him. Would Rohan's presence overshadow his chance with Sharvari? Amidst all this chaos of their intertwined lives, would he be impressing her?

In an empty house's silence, he sat there, and the echoes were what he would have—his future self warning him. Ghosts of regret, of missed chances loomed ahead of him, stretching out tentacles toward the still-fluttering hope of a better tomorrow. It was full of risks, with time running out like sand through his fingers.

It was here that young Vrushabh understood that the journey ahead would be tough; he would also have to fight the time-keeping commission and past demons of mistakes. The excitement of ambition wrestled with the burden of responsibility, and he felt love for Sharvari tugging at his soul, fighting against the wayward desires that had taken him far away.

Refreshed in his resolve, he vowed to drive through the confusion of feelings and ties. That annual fest would prove to be a turnaway for the rewriting of their lives. As he was getting ready for that function, that first flicker of hope began to ignite within—a feeling, perhaps, he could just hack it through on a road to redemption and a future with promises of being brighter.

It was in the quiet solitude of that empty house that young Vrushabh realised how difficult the journey ahead was going to be, but he stood ready to face it head-on. Where there were echoes of silence, a symphony of possibilities now emerged, and with open arms, he embraced that uncertainty and prepared himself against the ghosts of his past for the shaping of a new destiny.

VI

The annual fest part 1

Fest day transformed Newtech College, bedecked with lights that sparkled in the breeze. The atmosphere reverberated with throngs of students stringing up bright-hued stalls that each seemed to depict an eagle's nest of creative possibilities and zealousness. Mr Das, the dear dean, looked around at the arrangements with a full heart, for he witnessed the dedication of his students when they scurried about—each one engaged in their role to make the event a successful one.

A sumptuous red carpet lay in wait at the entrance for the exotic chief guest. Girls in their traditional attire shone brightly in their innocence, with sparkling eyes and bewitching hospitality, as they managed things along with Mr Kulkarni, whose very presence infused warmth and assurance to the festive spirit. The boys were busy organising the cultural and sporting activities that would feature during the program, with laughter echoing across the campus, creating an infectious sense of camaraderie.

Out of them, the earliest to arrive was Rohan. An upsurge of thrill mixed with responsibility hit as he started preparing for the drama show. His heart was physically pumped with ecstasy as he procured costumes for characters such as Kakbhushundi, envisaging what he could bring forth on the stage. The auditorium echoed with their collective energy as he called fellow actors who approached with faces emerging like sunflowers in late noon. It was then that Sharvari called his phone. Her wheelchair showed what tribulations she had gone through. Rohan responded

"Everything is ready! Why don't you come and see the final rehearsal before the play?" he insisted, his eyes filled with encouragement to see her.

"I would love to, but my wheelchair is causing me problems, and I have my grandmother along with me,"

she replied, her face shading with disappointment. Rohan felt empathy, wishing he could share her miseries and make her experience the joys of the fest as well.

Vrushabh was getting ready for the long-awaited college fest. His heart was racing with excitement, along with the slight fear of uncertainty. His future self turned toward the mirror to see that the block formation on his hand was spreading all over the body and reminding him of the challenges. He felt that the blocks were crawling on his face, creating a lot of pain on his face and making him worry. Suddenly, Vrushabh's future self appeared with an offer of a motorcycle ride to the college.

"Let's go!

You can't miss this fest", he said in a determined voice.

With every stride on their way, the wind was incessant, whipping his hair; for in that flicker of a moment, all worries blurred away. He parked his motorcycle, and his future self said,

"I'll just be here for the annual fest, you simply stay today to enjoy. Just be ready when Sharvari comes; this time, we will get the positions right!

As Rohan stepped completely into the preparation, the campus came alive with the students, their laughter echoing off every wall. He felt shivers of happiness at the thought of the performance. Friendship among the students was rampant in the air as each person turned out to be a part of the vibrant tapestry of the fest. Delicious street food cooked by peers wafted thick in the air, calling everyone to taste its appetising aroma.

The college glowed brilliant gold in the setting sun, and excitement was at its peak. Music and hooting fill the air as Rohan takes one moment and soaks in the beauty of that moment. He thought about Sharvari, wishing she could share this happy moment with him. He wanted to make the drama show a tribute to her spirits so that, despite her problems, she felt part of the celebration.

This festival was more or less like a fairy tale, and each of the events therein was a chapter of it, brimming with laughter, competition, and celebration. Students came out to show their talents: be it dance performances or sports competitions, every act an epitome of hard work and dedication. All this reverberated into cheers of good wishes, binding every being together.

Night had fallen, and the whole of the campus looked like a land of colours and lights. The moment he straddled the stage, his heart jumped with both elation and trepidation. He turned to the audience; his eyes naturally rested on Sharvari's grandmother, who was wheeling her in, a wide grin covering the latter's face. Suddenly, the adrenaline rushed into Rohan's head; this wasn't going to be an actual audience performance but a performance for Sharvari so she could realise she was meant to stay here with them.

Rohan flowed his heart into the characters with passion and grace. There was giggling and clapping, and audiences became spellbound in the auditorium. Rohan had a surge of fulfilment, feeling he was sharing something special with all of them.

The play soon began to unfold, holding the entire auditorium spellbound. Friends Shraddha, Devashri, Abhy, Vrushabh, and Mitesh were assembled, along with Sharvari, who elegant herself to the seating area in her wheelchair, guided by her grandma. The atmosphere was electric, the anticipation in the air was palpable.

The stage presented the ancient city of Ayodhya; its concept was based on an epic tale by Kakbhushundi and Garud in which a celestial eagle named Garuda mounts Shri Hari and flies with unparalleled strength. It was a classic epic play, knitting stories of valour and devotion that met with the knowledge of Kakbhushundi, and just after the flow of the story, there was applause from the audience, celebrating the dedication and talent of the cast.

Rohan, the scriptwriter, stood and watched with tears of joy glistening in his eyes. All this hard work had culminated in this beautiful moment, and the sight of his friends there to support him was overwhelming with pride. Finally, at the end of the last act, the college dean, Mr. Das, announced, "Everyone, all the fun fairs, stores, and every student activity is open for one and all to enjoy now!" The auditorium began getting ready with enthusiasm for the upcoming performances.

Rohan prepared himself to join the group—go for a look around in the carnival, but Sharvari, young blood pulsing through her veins, decided to be with her friends.

"Let me go, Dadiji!"

she repeated, her voice a blend of obstinacy and expectation. Her sensitive but protective grandmother retorted, "No need to go; we'll head home now.

The friends rallied around Sharvari; the camaraderie shone through. Vrushabh stepped forward, confidence radiating from him.

"I'll take her home," he offered, his eagerness palpable.

"I'll look after her."

Sharvari's grandmother hesitated, her face a mix of anger and concern. "But she should be home by 10 o'clock, or it won't be good for all of you," she warned, underlining the instinct to protect.

And the friends knew, as they looked at each other, it was a tightrope walk between freedom and responsibility. They assured Sharvari's grandmother that they would come back in time and take care of her. The joy bubble caressed them in the warmth of togetherness and clicked amidst the uncertainty; thereafter, they tumbled.

As the festival proceeded, there was lots of laughter and the sound of music. Rohan felt an upsurge of gratitude toward his friends who stood by him at all times. The thrill of drama turned out to be successful: mixed with the festive joy, it made the evening memorable.

Her laughter echoed through the exploration of the stalls, her spirits infectious. Stories were shared, and with each moment, bonds grew deeper. The festival was turning into a celebration of friendship, creativity, and the similitudes of life.

As 10 approached, the friends crowded around Sharvari, making sure that the grandmother felt at ease. They promised to return her home early enough. The sincerity was there in their voice. The grandmother watched the real care that was expressed by all of them and smiled a little.

"Alright, but be responsible," she finally relented, a hint of a smile breaking through her otherwise stern countenance.

So the friends, light in their hearts, full of laughter, skipped into the night, determinedly. The festival was not an event for them; to them, it was a tapestry of memories being woven—one thread after another, by one experience after another among themselves.

The air rang with excitement, and Rohan felt the union deeper than ever before. His script had brought them all together, and now, the light of their friendship guided him through. Like an island of vivid colours and sensory overloads, Rohan moved through the street even more confident that what was being paid was not merely an accolade for his work but an acknowledgement of the connections created.

And so the evening concluded in this wondrous melange of exultation, shared thankful sentiments, and warmth from friendship. Rohan was surrounded by his buddies, and he knew it. This was going to be that moment he would cherish forever—a successful drama but a real feeling of friendship, developed through the process of shared experience. As they strolled through the college fest, out unfolded a vivacious tapestry of local Indian street food stalls and a myriad of colourful gift shops, all tastefully arranged by the enthusiastic students.

The atmosphere was festive and abuzz with excitement, electrified further by the grandeur of the nearby standing palace that served as a majestic backdrop. The warm light of glittering light infused the atmosphere and was interspersed with merry sounds of laughter and chatter, creating an almost fairytale-like ambience.

Starting right from the entrance to the building, they were greeted by an attractive array of attractions promising adventure and delight. On every floor, there were interactive settings—ranging from terrifying horror houses that ran chills down the spine to the more inviting Japanese cafes that drew one like a magnet through the appetising aroma of food. Rohan helped Sharvari in her wheelchair from one engrossing experience to another, deftly guiding her with a light touch so she never felt left out. In this jarring crowd, the thorn of envy pierced Vrushabh's heart as Roahn and Sharvari were coming closer, their laughter intermingling like a sweet melody.

They resolved to have the shrikhand dessert on the third and topmost floor, one of Sharvari's favourite desserts. This creamy sweet one was a perfect way to celebrate their special day. And with each bite, the tastes began to dance on their tongues—childhood memories of family reunions flooded back. At a Japanese-themed coffee shop, Shraddha and Abhay gorged on sushi of all types, learning about new ones, and each taste made their eyes sparkle. It created an air of discovery that bound them all in communal joy.

In the jamboree, Mitesh's heart thumped as his eyes fell on Devshri, resplendent in her pink traditional saree. There was something in her that seemed to light up the room, but seeing her, he felt a surging of emotions: admiration, longing, and a hint of nostalgia. There was something about her that reminded him of all those moments of laughter they shared and the secrets they exchanged—most of which he couldn't brush aside.

It was not an event, but a celebration of life, friendship, and the beautiful tapestry of experiences connecting all. The laughter echoed down the halls, mingling with tantalising smells of street food and brilliant colours of decorations. Every moment stood testament to the bonds shared.

From one event to another, each experience further etched their bonding. Rohan and Sharvari's laughter was like music to the ears, filling up the air with warmth. Vrushabh found himself smiling amidst his envy at their joy, realising how often the blossoming of friendship came about through unexpected ways. Shraddha and Abhay were engrossed in their culinary adventure. Quips were exchanged with banter that was infectious in its joy.

It was more than a festival. The college fest stood as an emotional kaleidoscope—nostalgia and enthusiasm. It reminded the girls that, much like the kiosks and sports that formed a perimeter around them, life was teeming with colours, flavours, and moments etched in their hearts. As they meandered through the festivities, they loved not just the experiences but the bonds that grew stronger with each shared smile and laughter.

By the end of the college building, Mitesh found himself flush with guts. With a racing heart, he turned to face Devashri; his cheeks had reddened.

"I want to talk about something,"

he stammered, totally off guard. She smiled, "Okay, tell me,"

but he hesitated,

"Not here, just come with me for a moment."

They stepped aside; their friends' eyes glued on them, curiosity bubbling in the air.

Vrushabh, curious, asked,

"What is it about?"

Shraddha, a mix of excitement and annoyance, replied, "Don't get between them, you idiot."

Abhy and Shraddha exchanged glances, anticipation etched on their faces, while Rohan and Sharvari remained oblivious to the unfolding drama.

Mitesh stood before Devashri, trembling and blushing, his heart pounding like a drum.

"I wanted to tell you for so long that I like you,"

he confessed, his voice barely audible.

"Would you want to go out with me? "

Devashri's smile faltered slightly.

"As friends, I like you," she replied gently, but Mitesh sensed hesitation in her tone.

"No, I want us to be more than just friends,"

he pressed on, hope flickering in his eyes.

The expression on Devashri's face changed.

"I can't be with you because I like someone else,"

she said softly, a hint of regret in her voice.

"We can just be friends."

The impact of her words descended upon Mitesh with the force of crushing weight; his heart was shattered into a million pieces. A pallor washed over his face, and sadness was etched deeply in his features.

She saw his distress and stepped in to lighten the situation.

"Hey, don't be down! Let us take some pictures,"

she said, trying to return the laughter. Vrushabh lay thinking about how he was going to approach Sharvari. His heart was racing at the urge to win her over.

It was followed by a beeline run of both, first taking pictures in front of the glowing billboards, then lifting the sign "I love Newtech College." The boys burst into laughter, but still, Mitesh's heart was heavy. They took turns clicking single snaps, making those unforgettable moments, but Mitesh still felt he was like a ghost among them—his spirit was dim.

Finally, he summoned the required courage and went to Sharvari.

"Why don't we try some fancy eating or some kinda game?"

he proposed, his heart racing. Sharvari's face brightened.

"Yes, we must try something new and exciting," she replied, turning to Rohan for suggestions. At this, Vrushabh's heart sank a bit—he couldn't help but feel a little envious about this easy rapport Rohan shared with her.

Amidst the repartee, Abhy felt a sudden intruder in the blackness of some corner or another, but it must have been an optical illusion. The group kept arguing animatedly; their peals of laughter and bonhomie slowly chipped away at Mitesh's depression, though the stinging sensation did not quite abate.

While they continued the walk to the horror house, the atmosphere was inhaled with excitement. Mitesh still bled from his unwrapped wounds, so he was trying to grab the moment with his friends. The thought of facing his fears with these people brought flashes of joy again to his heart.

"Let's make it a night to be remembered!"

Shraddha declared, rallying everyone. Mitesh couldn't help but smile as he got infected by her enthusiasm. Entering the horror house with screams and laughter intermingled in darkness, they met with surprises at each corner, jumping and laughing together.

It was then, surrounded by companions and the element of surprise, that Mitesh realised that, though his heart was aching, there was some pleasure to be had in friendship and shared experience. The night unfolded in unexpected ways with laughter ringing down the corridors, and for a moment, the pain of rejection faded into the background.

As they came out of the house of horrors, breathing and elated, Mitesh felt a resurgence of hope. Maybe it wasn't the end; perhaps it was the beginning. He could face whatever came his way—a step at a time—now that he had his friends to share in the austerity of the moment with the embedded thought that joy could still be found amidst heartache.

To ease up the mood, they decided to experience a horror house that was organised by Shraddha's classmate, which Abhy was overjoyed with. The air in the horror house hung heavy, like a second skin, with dread so palpable it dripped into the pores. The flickering dim lights—casting deep pools of shadow into the rooms—sent shivers racing down their spines. This hush, with horror, increased the clammy creaking of the woodwork and far-off moans, which were like the reminder, one by one, of malevolent spirits that seemed to lurk just out of sight.

Farther inside, the air grew dense with a sense of heaviness. The floors were crawling with zombies—bodies filled up the meagerly lit hallways. The lighting created a peculiar sheen on such grotesque features. It seemed like, in places, some bodies slightly twitched, holding on to the last threads of life, but in others, organisms rested placidly with eyes as hollow as the depths. All this was so lifelike that it just seemed that at any moment, the dead could rise and take the living with them into their eternal sleep.

And then, just from within the shadows, a werewolf emerged with a feral glow in its eyes. Towering muscle rippled beneath its matted fur, and it growled through flesh and bone, returning an echoing growl that chilled to the bone of those who beheld the sight. Above, in the darkness, the vampires flitted by in their capes—a cloud of darkness gliding with an undertone of whispered promises and chilling laughter. Small monsters scurried around at their feet, their claws adding to the cacophony of terror that surrounded them.

Through all this chaos, Sharvari suddenly burst with fear. Her heart thumped like a drum in her chest as she stumbled through the darkness. In her falling, she accidentally grasped Rohan's hand, a moment of unexpected connection amidst the horror. The warmth of his grip gave her a momentary feeling of safety, but it was superseded by the sight of Vrushabh, his face contorted with rage and envy.

"May I?"

Vrushabh said, dripping sarcasm.

"Hold Sharvari's wheelchair now?

You must be tired, Rohan.".

Rohan was not going to be put off so easily. He responded with assurance, "No, I'm not tired. I can handle it." His voice was as solid as the stormy world swarming about them. The tension between the three was palpable; a silent war being played in the middle of the horror show.

Further and further, the helplessness was gripping Vrushabh in the strangest of ways. He watched Abhy and Shraddha as they held hands, laughing, and their echoes in the darkened halls were in sharp contrast to his fear. There was a vague sensation of being shadowed tickling at the back of his mind, and the hairs on the nape of his neck stood on end.

By now, Mitesh and Devashri had reached an awkward silence—an aura of unannounced words waiting to be said by her for his rejection. The buzzing chaos became somewhat distant as two people engaged in their acrimony, while the laughter around them dissolved into a haunting echo.

Shraddha, as ever, was one for having a bit of fun. She began making a game of all the different mascots that adorned her way out. Laughing, she poked and prodded the creepy figures; her laughter lit the darkness like an angler's beacon against old curses. Under her fingers, each of these mascots sprang to life; their painted smiles contrasted sharply with the horror that surrounded them.

That student-run haunted house was a complex interweaving of fear and excitement, meant to elicit from the visitor equal proportions of scream and laughter. Full of energy, the walls pulsed with each scare waiting around every corner, ready to be revealed. It made a great horror show, crossing over to the fantastic but leaving all in attendance breathless and wide-eyed with horror.

The nearer they came to the exit, the dimmer the flickering lights, casting long shadows that almost contorted like spectres on the walls. The cacophony reached a near-deafening crescendo, a symphony of shock that would echo in their minds long after they left. The high of the fear mixed with the glee over shared experience would create a bond between them that would outlast the ending of a long night. End of the night, as it was 9 p.m., they had just come from that moment of darkness.

And Abhy began giving directions towards the exit. As Abhy and his friends came out of the college building, he had that vibe again. He looked around and froze the moment with his friends in his mind. Vrushabh was standing a little away from Rohan, who was pushing Sharvari's wheelchair, and Mitesh lurked behind, as usual, awkwardly. Devshri and Shraddha were engrossed in a hushed conversation and were completely oblivious to the danger.

Abhy's heart raced at the thought of the dark shadow that had been following them. His worst fears were realised as the air was pierced by the deafening gunshot. Time froze as Abhy looked in horrified screams, "No!" as the bullet whizzed to meet Rohan in the head. The impact was devastating, and Rohan crumpled lifeless to the ground.

From out of the darkness, a figure emerged to present a view that did little but turn his blood cold: older Arushi, speaking into a communication device. "The first anomaly is dead," she said with a voice full of malice. Out of the dark, from all around the campus, began materialising the members of the TKC. The laughter from Arushi came as she said,

"Found you!"

The badness of it all was etched on their faces, and panic set into the group. They turned to run as Sharvari had been devastated by Rohan's death. She refused to leave as her cries resounded in the air, begging Vrushabh,

"Why don't you do something?"

Vrushabh, really somehow dodging Arushi's bullets at full sprint while pushing Sharvari in her wheelchair, felt torn between wanting to flee and needing to comfort his friend.

The group ran helter-skelter in the chaos, their hearts racing with fear and adrenaline. Abhy's mind raced against time as he tried to process the unbelievable events that had just transpired. Rohan, their friend and confidant, was no more—his life snuffed out by a callous twist of fate.

As they fled, Abhy knew not how to shake off that guilt within. Had he been more vigilant in his environs, perhaps he could have averted this disaster. Rohan's death burrowed into him and became a weight he would carry to his grave.

Everywhere, the members of the TKC chased them, the sound of their footsteps in the deserted campus. Abhy and his friends ran for their lives. Lungs were flying with every desperate breath; if they got caught, their fate would be sealed, going with Rohan in the cruel embrace of death.

Rounding a corner, Abhy had a glimpse of Arushi's distorted face, her eyes flashing malevolently, obviously enjoying this, wallowing in the chaos and terror she'd unleashed. His blood boiled with rage, but he knew this wasn't the time for vengeance. Their only hope was in flight, to live another day and somehow find how to put a stop to Arushi and these other TKC monsters.

The group ran—legs aching, hearts heavy with grief and fear. Yet deep inside, they knew they were running not for their lives but to save the future from the TKC, which had come out in its true colours, leaving Abhy and his friends as the last ones who could stop them from changing the course of history forever.

The memory of Rohan was burned bright in their minds, fleeing into the unknown, reminding them of how fragile life is and that one needs to enjoy the present moment. They knew they would carry his spirit in them, lighting up in darkness that threatened to consume them all.

VII

The annual fest part 2

On their flight from Arushi, the group stumbled into an empty classroom; the door creaked ominously behind them. Dimly lit, the moonlight had passed through the windows and left long, dark shadows along the floor, dancing. They took refuge behind the sturdy wooden desk, a barrier between them and the chaos in the streets. There was a very close air filled with tension and fear itself.

Sharvari sat there in her wheelchair, her face an epitome of agony, tears shining in her eyes as she mourned the untimely death of Rohan. She could see flashes of his laughter and warmth infiltrating her mind—each memory was as though a vacuum cleaner had been shown how to clean with full vacuum power. She felt like a part of her had been ruthlessly ripped off, making her hollow and sore. The world outside seemed so far away, muffled by the walls of that classroom, but the ache within her was too real to be ignored.

At her side, Shraddha bent forward. Her voice became tender, a whisper to try to comfort her friend.

"Sharvari, I know it hurts. We'll get through this together,"

she said, her heart heavy with sorrow. She reached out and put a reassuring hand on Sharvari's shoulder, trying—to translate the strength she felt slipping onto the other side. Shraddha had red-rimmed eyes, showing her battle not to let go—the loss seemed stifling, but still, she knew they had to be strong for each other.

Abhy, in the multi-tasks he always did, had one eye on the door. He could feel the tension of their silence, used to comment—the realisation of the danger outside. It was not only his heart filled with fear but also with the overwhelming responsibility for his friends.

"Let's stay focused,"

he underlined again, with his voice holding steady against the chaos in his head. "If we panic, we'll lose our chance to escape."

His eyes scoured the room for the slightest movement as his mind raced through strategies that would get them out alive.

Mitesh and Devashri sat together, their faces reflecting a jumble of emotions: confusion and sadness. They couldn't understand the reasons, or at least the extent to which they had feelings for this man, Rohan, who had been their friend, their confidant, their shining star-bearer through life's dark times. They were still aware of his absence, and they would look at one another with silent questions in their eyes.

"Where do we even start to make sense of this?"

Mitesh finally ventured, his voice hardly more than a whisper.

Devashri just shook her head as tears coursed down her face because the words she searched for would not come. Vrushabh stood at the corner of the room, his eyes tear-soaked, his face a picture of desperation. He felt the almost unbearable urge to reach out to his soulmate in this future, who would bring relief and deliver appropriate guidance during such uncertain times.

"Why can I not just call him?"

he almost spat as frustration built up inside. To be kept in this moment and not be able to seek answers was agonising. He felt he was drowning in an ocean of despair, with each wave pulling him further under. Assuming that all happened because of TKC, which came due to him and his future self's actions, Vrushabh said,

"Everything will be fine, don't you worry, guys,"

trying to muster a sense of hope for his friends. He wanted to believe his own words, but doubt gnawed at him. Sharvari, her eyes drenched with pain, wheeled closer to him, her voice shaking.

"Don't you feel something?

Don't you sense the weight of this loss?

" Her words tore through the fragile pretence of calm he was trying to maintain.

"Don't say that!"

Shraddha interposed, the concern evident. She looked at the lines of pain on Sharvari's face and felt her own heart clenching in pain.

"We need to hold on to hope, not let despair consume us."

The urgency in her voice was but a reflection of her fears, a plea for strength amidst the chaos.

"Yeah, I do,"

Vrushabh admitted in a hush.

"But you won't get it."

Even he was taken aback by the tone of his voice, the velvety edge displaying how deeply frustrated he was. The balance was hard; he was stuck between needing to give comfort to his friends and the reality of the situation. "Stay calm," Abhy reassured: his composure was a lighthouse in the tempest of emotions that had just raged by. "We should support each other in this tough time." His words conjured up a sense of togetherness, a sense of not being alone, but in all of this together. He inhaled deeply to calm himself down; his friends expected this from him.

But as the tension mounted in the darkened room, Vrushabh made a desperate call to his future self, but the network signal was at its weakest, so the call was dropped. When the group huddled in terror, the sound of approaching footsteps was really in the classroom. Abhy sensed the impending danger and dragged Shraddha closer, pointing other students to hide, as the most dangerous intruder entered clad in the most terrible military-grade armour.

The presence of the intruder had been overwhelming, and the footsteps only served to exacerbate the chills running through their spines. Mitesh, hidden along with Devshri, felt that intrusive gaze was concentrating like a spotlight on him and, quite subconsciously, braced for impact. Much like an animal, in a purely instinctive moment, Abhy lunged forward and faced the intruder rather fiercely.

"I'm not here to harm you!"

The words barked at the intruder, but anger quickly turned to hostility as he punished Abhy's face with a vicious blow.

"Why are you here?"

Abhy demanded, his voice creaking with wrath. The garbed man now introduced himself: His name was Joy, and he was a time enforcer.

"I'm here to capture anomalies in the timeline caused by humans,"

he said.

Abhy was taken aback and was about to tumble when Joy instantly took the opportunity of this weakness and sent Abhy down with an adrenaline blow. Then he captured Abhy with others. Just when Joy was about to reveal his discoveries to the TKC members, all of a sudden there occurred a hullabaloo. Future Vrushabh appeared out of the blue with a rod made of steel and hit Joy on his head and he fainted.

Chaos erupted in the room as they identified the Future Vrushabh, as he was called by the group—Mohit: their saviour. Now in fevered blood, they all grabbed hold of each other yet again as realisation hit them on the face hard. Mohit explained the timeline disturbances and the dire consequences in case Joy succeeded in his mission.

As the realisation sunk in, they picked themselves off the mat and rushed out of the classroom to face whatever anomalies stood in the way of their existence. United in fear but filled with determination, the group was in ready mode for the battles that lay ahead, as they could very well sense their very survival was at stake if they could not unite and fight impending doom: Joy and the disruptions within their timeline.

Mohit stood firm, his heart racing as he turned toward the mess that was going on around him. That classroom, which used to be a den of learning, had now been reduced to a cage. Everywhere were the officers of TKC; their presence looming. He pointed out the critical condition they were in, and he felt his friend's fear through his eyes—an image of his turmoil.

The blocks of infection, glowing, now spreading on the face of Mohit, mesmerised Vrushabh as a manifestation of the risk they were in. Light pulsing resonated with increasing urgency in his mind, telling him to leave that place. The tension was broken by Mohit's voice, telling them to hurry.

"Follow my lead,"

he ordered, trying to sound as commanding as possible while containing desperation. Crouched low and stepping wordlessly, his eyes open for enemies, Mohit followed up at the rear. The weight of the package in his pocket seemed to grow heavier with each step, reminding him of what he had stolen from Arushi and who he was with—the burden of the key to the time machine.

It was in the quiet of that empty room that Mohit turned to Vrushabh with a serious expression.

"Take this,"

he said, handing over the package.

"Open it only when you need me the most."

Thus, with a little more than a gleam of hope and a glimpse of something potentially wonderful, the fourth dimension key did gleam at him through the poor light.

"I can't do this,"

Vrushabh protested, his voice trembling.

"I can't even manage to impress Sharvari."

He felt the weight of expectations crashing down on him, the pressure to succeed in a world that seemed to conspire against him.

"No,"

Mohit insisted, his voice straining with effort, yet firm.

"I know I have so much potential. You can be anything that you want to be. Just believe in yourself."

The glowing blocks on his skin pulsed brighter—a bodily reminder of the slipping away of time. But "Where did you hide the package for this many days," Vrushabh asked.

"It was in the drawer below the TV",

Mohit replied.

While they stood up and turned to leave, the real realisation of all that was happening suddenly crashed upon Vrushabh. The fear of defeat gnawed at him, but Mohit's unfaltering belief ignited a flicker of hope within his heart. "What if I can't make everything right?"

he whispered, doubt crawling into his heart.

His eyes turned soft, infused with pain and a look of determination.

"You have to try," he pleaded.

"You have to believe in yourself, even when it feels impossible.

With that, they fell in line behind the friends of Vrushabh, the weight of their mission almost palpable on their shoulders. Each step felt like a jump into the unknown. It was a heady mix of fear and hope. Mohit's heart was racing fast, not because of danger lurking around the corner but because he was putting his future in somebody else's hands.

As they swooped in through the shadows, the world out beyond seemed at a far remove, an echo perhaps of the turmoil within. Mohit's thoughts raced; were they going to make it? Would Vrushabh show up this time? Stakes were high, and the pressure was suffocating.

The sudden, jarring noise cut through an otherwise silent night, reminding him that danger was never far behind. Mohit's instincts kicked in, and he instinctively pushed Vrushabh and the others ahead.

"Go! Now!" he shouted, urgency lacing his voice.

They continued running, the adrenaline making tugs on them as Mohit just watched ahead, his heart bumping in rhythm with the glowing blocks on his skin. Each pulse now started to feel like a countdown, as a reminder that time was running out.

It was when they began running up and down the corridors that their bonding did. Mohit's belief in Vrushabh had become a life jacket, the thread between them in the madness.

"You can do this,"

he whispered, though it was more to himself than to Vrushabh.

They walked carefully, aware of the threats each member of TKC posed in these dimly lit corridors of the college building. Devshri expertly steered Sharvari's wheelchair while her heart raced with every sound echoing from the walls. Abhy, Shraddha, and Mitesh trailed closely behind, their eyes nervously darting around; Mohit and Vrushabh brought up the back, looking for any trouble that could happen.

A tense moment developed as they reached near the exit. The group has already begun exchanging anxiety-laden stares with one another, gesturing at silent reminders to become very vigilant. Abhy took the lead; his pulse was racing as he approached the exit gate, and he felt relieved for a second. From the dark corners, out came Aarushi as if she emerged like a ghost from the depths of earth and hell combined. Her eyes gleamed with evil intentions. She delivered a flying kick at Abhy, sending him down to the ground.

"Get up!" Sharvari shouted in a panic as Aarushi whipped out a gun, pointing directly at Devshri. The air thickened with menace as TKC guys began materialising out of the dark and surrounded them, their intentions plain as daylight.

"Your time is up,"

Aarushi sneered, her finger itching frighteningly close to the trigger. Finally, as she jerked the gun backwards, Mitesh propelled himself between Devshri and the bullet.

"No!"

Devshri screamed, her heart coming apart as Mitesh took the hit, collapsing to the ground.

"Why did you save me?"

she wept, flying right back to his side, her hands shaking as she cradled his head. Mitesh, failing fast, did turn up a weak grin.

"Because I love you, idiot," he whispered before his eyes fluttered shut and he fell unconscious.

Aarushi's expression changed to one of triumph, replacing the previous shock. "Oh, shit, he wasn't an anomaly,"

she muttered, a touch of disappointment in her voice. She described her alignment with the D-division of TKC, a group that had as its primary objective the disintegration of timelines irreconcilable in nature. The "D" in it stood for death, quite literally; the mission, set. Eliminate any threats to the objectives at hand.

"Just let you guys get demonstrated,"

she ordered, her voice cold and commanding. The TKC members tightened their grip on the group; all faces turned completely devoid of empathy. "Bring him to me," Aarushi commanded, pointing at Mr. Kulkarni, who was dragged forward, bound and helpless.

With a flick of her wrist, Aarushi drew from her pocket a cube-like device whose surface glowed ominously. She set it on Kulkarni's head, and he was immediately reduced to a nebula of radiant dust. In a moment, everything about him evaporated, leaving behind nothing but a vague, haunting echo of existence. Devshri gasped. The horror of it all came crashing down on her like a tidal wave.

"Why are you doing this?"

Abhy croaked, struggling to rise. He could hardly speak above a whisper. Aarushi turned, her eyes glinting with a mix of cruelty and resolution. "Because you are all a threat to the balance of time. You don't understand what's at stake here."

The realisation hit the remaining members as the reality of their predicament finally set in. They were trapped—caught in a web spun by some ruthless organisation that saw them only as pawns in some giant game.

"Devshri, we gotta get out of here!"

Mohit said, his voice urgent now. But the TKC closed in; their faces tightened in anticipation of doing the deed that Aarushi had instructed them to do. The atmosphere was heavy with tension, and desperation weighed heavily upon this little group.

"Think, think!"

Shraddha whispered loudly, while her mind raced feverishly for a solution.

"We can't let this be the end!"

Just at that moment, Mitesh stirred. His eyelids fluttered open, and he gasped, "We can't give up. We fight back,"

His voice was very weak but determined.

With a renewed spirit, the group assembled again; the fear was now etched on their faces and replaced by a mad terror to be free of TKC. They knew they had to act fast; their lives hung in a precarious balance. As they calculated the plan, the shadows all around them almost pulsed ominously, but they would be ready for whatever was to come. Mohit's voice was clear and authoritative, yelling at Vrushabh to open the package and hand it over. The TKC crowded in close around Sharvari's wheelchair, their eyes darting nervously, knowing the tension that hung like a pall of air. Mitesh lay, unconscious, a little distance away, an unfortunate casualty of what was going on.

Vrushabh followed the order, tearing open the packet to reveal a beautiful 144 mm handgun, made of gold and fully loaded. It was such a dangerous well of beauty. Vrushabh, expressionless, tossed the gun toward Mohit, who caught it expertly with his finger itching on the trigger as he pointed it menacingly at Arashi.

The opportune moment finally came when Abhy charged forward, only to be met by a powerful kick to the face, which sent him flying backwards. As he regained his stance, he threw a similar cube at her. She dodged well, and the cube struck a TKC member, who instantly turned into ash. "Aren't you a fast one?" Arushi taunted, oozing confidence.

"You ain't seen anything fast yet,"

Abhy shot back, launching himself on her again, this time powered by adrenaline and rage.

Mohit and Vrushabh fought valiantly against the closing members of the TKC. Both of them moved as one unit, keeping the attackers at bay with all their might, making sure that Sharvari and Devashri were safe. The tension was palpable. Every punch and gunshot resounded like thunder in that enclosed space.

Shraddha crept behind Arushi, moving undulating with grace, and aimed a kick at her. But then Arushi turned around, unfazed, and dispatched a quick back kick, sending Abhy crashing to the ground for the second time. The fight was getting fiercer, and the stakes were higher than ever before.

Then, in a shocking turn of events, Arushi seized Shraddha by the neck and easily lifted her with the gun pressed against her forehead. "Any last words?" she sneered.

"Y-you're a crazy bi—"

Shraddha managed to stammer before Arashi pulled the trigger. The gunshot came like a knell as Shraddha dropped lifelessly to the ground. Blood from the wound sprayed out of her body as she fell. Her eyes were wide open, brimming with shock.

Enraged by the brutal killing of his beloved, Abhy erupted in anger. He sprang to his feet, and a wild scream emerged from his lips while he rushed toward Arushi to avenge Shraddha's death. But with icy precision, Arushi aimed at him; her finger already poised over the trigger, the shot resounded in chorus with the bedlam, and Abhy collapsed lifeless to the floor, his hand still outstretched toward Shraddha.

Seeing the carnage, a few of the TKC members began to hesitate; their resolve was waning as fear seeped into their ranks. Mohit and Vrushabh launched a counter-attack with renewal of energy on the remaining ones. Metallic blood and acrid gunpowder—the stench hung in the air; every moment seemed to ratchet up the tension.

She stood amidst all the chaos—her face a mixed bag of triumph and madness. Surveying the scene, Arushi looked at the fallen bodies of Abhay and Shraddha and the terrified faces of the TKC. "You think you can stop me?"—she taunted, her voice dripping in contempt.

Vrushabh glared at her with an aggressive breath.

"This isn't over, Arushi. We will fight till our last breath."

"Is that a promise?"

she sneered back with an ill-intended half-smile.

What followed was the regrouping by the TKC members, now devoid of some of the fear and motivated by desperate determination. They charged at them; Mohit and Vrushabh were waiting. Flaying bodies moved in fluid, practised motions as each punch thrown was for the friends they lost, and each dodge was a testament to their will.

The battle raged on, a dance of chaos, violence, and desperation. Now trapped, Arushi drew out yet another weapon; her eyes shone with madness. "You think you can take me down? Ha! I'm just getting started! Looking at Mohit.

Mohit roared,

"It's between you and me!"

as he stood squared off against Arashi. Their fists clashed with immense force, echoes of which reverberated amidst the chaos all around. The punches, each one like an adrenaline rush, crunched through in crackling air. Arushi taunted in a voice full of contempt:

"You know what you are doing, timeline corruptor!

And suddenly, she blew with great force as Mohit was pushed back and thrown to the ground. He attempted to rise, but Arushi had pulled out a timeline extractor. Evil light radiated from the instrument, imbuing her with determination. She switched it on, and rays swept over Mohit, tearing at his very being, leaving him as cubic, glowing crystals that threatened to tear reality's fabric itself apart.

"Stop!" Vrushabh tried to shout desperately, coming in between, his heart pounding away. "I would give you the time-machine key; only let him free."

"Are you kidding?" Arushi stopped right in front, her hand at the extractor, wavering. "Then just let him go!" Vrushabh lashed out loud with his voice filled with urgency, and anger since Mohit was becoming visibly dim.

"Don't allow her to get it! It's our last chance!" Mohit gasped, the expression on his face in shrill pain as he fought the suction of the extractor.

Vrushabh's power ebbed away. "I can't help it! All our friends are dead!" His voice broke, and he threw the key towards Arushi with a toss of his hand.

"You are good, but I'm not," she spoke coldly and reignited the extractor. He heard a whir as the device came to life, and his future self shredded into nothing. What remained was his clothes and bike key, a ghostly remnant of loss.

And despair bombarded Mohit as the light enveloped him. "You can't, Vrushabh!" he screamed, but it was too late. The timeline extractor stepped up the tempo of its hum, dragging out its last final shimmers of existence, leaving silence in the wake of the titanic struggle. Vrushabh was shocked, rooted to the spot in despair, as wave after wave of despair smote him. TKC members had taken Dishe, and Sharvari fell from her wheelchair, crying in despair. It was as though he could feel the last iota of hope ebbing out of him, just like sand falling out of one's grip.

"Just kill me now," he had said with deep sorrow in his eyes at Arashi. She now turned the gun at him, still having that cold look on her face. "Nah, you should die with this timeline," she said, taking the weapon away from him and activating the glowing cube, which started eating everything in its way. The TKC members vanished finally in their circular time machine along with Sharvari, and Vrushabh found himself left all alone in a gloomful abyss.

Devshri approached him, her voice in a quiver, yet firm. "Don't just give up. You have to save us! I don't know what's going on, but I know you can fix this." Her words pierced through his desolation like a dagger, hitting a flicker of determination in him. "Easy for you to say," he said under his breath, overcome with feelings of inadequacy.

Devshri looked at him fiercely and reminded him of their childhood bond. "We have been friends since childhood, and I have loved you. Indeed, I have." She hung her declaration in midair, a lifeline thrown into a sea of his hopelessness. "I have got no power, but I want it all. I do not know, but only dreams. Nothing I can do, but I slog for nothing!" His voice cracked; the desperation was palpable.

"'If you can do anything you would like to do,' she said, and slapped him back into reality with a dramatic slap, 'I don't know what you're going to do, but save us all!" And with that, something began to burn deep in him here: something that drove him to where the keys lay, on the ground of a former college campus that was falling apart around him, the painted wails of students in his ears.

He started his bike, and the rush of adrenaline just overpowered his senses. Every faction of the rising RPM was a pulse in his heart, carrying him faster and faster toward the unknown. Memories of laughter and friendship became interwoven with the turmoil of the present, each fueling his resolve. He wasn't just racing time; he was racing for his life.

And as he pulled away from the scene, a burdened past seemed to pass it and collide with the uncertainty of the future. The faces of his friends flashed before his eyes—hopes and dreams all intertwined with his own. He could not let them down. He would not let despair win.

In every twist of the throttle, he felt the burden of doubt lifts slightly from his shoulders. That bike became an extension of my very will—an inanimate vessel carrying the determination to change the course of fate. Whizzing on the bike, under the shimmering night sky, Vrushabh attained breakneck speed toward the towering mountain where the ancient temple of Shiva lay. The wind raced through his hair as the thrill of approaching the holy site surged within him. The mountain loomed large, impregnable—a dark sentinel against the twinkling stars, speaking in hushed tones as secret as those it alone knew from the divine.

Walking towards the premises of the temple, there was Kakbhushundi's mystic pond, its waters shining like liquid silver. Legends spoke of its power to bend time, yet all that magnetised Vrushabh. He turned back, and the mountain, along with all else, began to dissolve into shimmering cubes, a kaleidoscope of reality unravelling before his eyes. This dreamlike metamorphosis nurtured a faith within Kakbhushundi, in the time-travel potency, boiling within him like a cocktail potion, feelings of hope and trepidation

With a heavy heart, Vrushabh jumped into the pool, the chill waters wrapping him around, like an envelope. Then, all at once, all was quiet—the second he was submerged, he found the world above, sucked into a deep silence, which echoed the wisdom of the monument. Beneath him, the crows circled, weaving intricate patterns within the darkness, which was now scarce since the moonlight beamed. They repeated their calls; the cawing seemed a chant encouraging him on, towards the miraculous change he desired.

Hours appeared to melt and flex in that pond. A light of memories began to flicker, fireflies in the dark, each one a shard of his expedition. He remembered the strife, the instances of hesitation, and the endless search for meaning that brought him here. Water undulated around him, shimmering not only with his likeness but the very nature of his desires and fears.

A jolt of energy ran through his body, and he felt an unseen force drawing him deeper into the pond's depths. The crows above increased their circling, their wings beating in sync with his racing heart. He almost felt their thoughts, urging him to let go of his earthly ties and embrace the unknown. The air filled with an unsuspecting sense of wanting, and the water started to shine, lighting the way ahead.

As he let the current wash over him, visions came to him from another age: the temple at its height, filled with worshippers praying for the blessings of Shiva. Within their hopes and prayers, he felt this weight of a collective yearning that reached across time. It was no mere pond but a portal to the past, a bridge to the divine.

VIII

Back from the future

The next moment, Vrushabh opened his eyes; he disbelieved himself. He was lying in his house exactly three days before the annual fest; he remembered nothing other than the magic of that pond. He picked up his mobile, to contact his future self, but as usual, it remained silent.

He searched everywhere. Rohan, alive and energetic, was found after hours, moving toward Sharvari's house. Vrushabh caught him up in a tight hug, and an overdose of happiness and relief filled his heart. "What's wrong with you?"

Rohan said in a surprising tone.

"Nothing, just missed you, my friend,"

said Vrushabh with a choked voice, and teary eyes that were holding tears themselves.

"Can I accompany you to her place?"

he said boldly, heart racing with thrilling enthusiasm. Rohan grinned,

"Why not? She will love it.

" Confusion flickered in Vrushabh's eyes.

"What do you mean?" Rohan teased.

"You will soon see!"

They reached Sharvari's villa, where she welcomed them with open arms; her grandmother was out, stuffing the place with young energy. Magic on Sharvari's face worked the moment Vrushabh stepped in.

"Why don't we show him our time dilater?"

she said mischievously, fidgeting in her wheelchair.

"You know we've been working on it since our trip to the temple."

The mention of time dilater stirred some very deep emotions into Vrushabh. By the sound of the words, images of their TKC and Arushi ran on his head, for Rohan and Sharvari moments tinged with laughter and camaraderie.

Theirs was a project; Sharvari enunciated, and in her eyes was laid a sparkle from the burning excitement,

"We believe that it may help us understand time even better—to live through moments we thought we had lost."

Her passion reignited the flame in Vrushabh's own heart, reminding him of the memories of their erstwhile dreams.

He added,

"Imagine if I could relive these favourite memories now, or maybe even a sneak peek into the future!"

The thought excited Vrushabh, but sadness now mingled with it. What if this was just a moment in time? What if he couldn't get this time back?

That certainly would have been a burst of laughter; it would have filled the room with light, with warmth. They would recount times spent in childhood reminiscing about their playful, sometimes not-so-innocent follies. Every story was a thread, sewing them even closer, a tapestry of shared experiences that would bind them to each other forever.

Yet, behind the façade, there was Vrushabh with his truth. Well, I was here after all, but until when? The urgency that something hanging in the future was around coursed through him, a shadow he couldn't shake off his conception of himself. He wanted to warn them, to protect them from the pain he knew lay ahead.

The dipping sun, sinking the golden flavour right into the walls of the villa, made him feel a surge of determination. Vrushabh would make the best of time, every laugh, every second spent with his friends. He would create new memories to hold on to, ones that could withstand the test of time.

"Let's make this a day to remember,"

he declared, and firmly. Rohan and Sharvari nodded. The smiles passed on. They experimented with the time dilater that evening; laughter filled the corridors, each moment a precious gift.

The warmth of the dying sun doused the streaks of the skies ever so slowly, making it look as though the sun wanted to embrace the entire city within its warm light, and Vrushabh and Rohan decided to take a leisurely walk home. These two friends had spent a wonderful evening with their friend Sharvari, sharing stories and laughter that would go on until the late hours of the night. But now, walking alongside each other through that well-trodden path, Vrushabh just couldn't shake the feeling of apprehension that had begun to stir and grow inside him.

He had harboured a secret—his genie weighed him bullishly right from the very first instance he met the notorious silhouette going by the nomenclature of Funter. To Vrushabh, it was clear as the cajole of bells signalling the cherished moment to open up and breathily share this onerous secret with one of his unbeatable buddies, Rohan, come what may, even if it meant a rather discouraged and shattered possibility of the real rage of his bosom friend, Rohan, given his sceptical temperament.

"Hey there, Rohan,"

Vrushabh started, nearly choking with his voice cracking a bit to indicate he was nervous.

"There is something important that I need to share with you, and I want you to promise me sincerely that you will listen throughout my little speech to the very end, regardless of how outlandish or unbelievable it may sound."

Rohan, understanding the gravity in Vrushabh's tone, nodded solemnly.

"Of course, man. You know you can tell me anything."

Vrushabh inhaled deeply by filling his lungs and then started narrating his intricately interwoven, gripping, and tension-filled story. He narrated his extraordinary experience with the Funter, the weird and mysterious thing that had exceptionally taken him centuries ahead in time, where he had been witness to the freakish events that one would never have imagined seeing. He described with utmost intensity Arushi's terrible, violent attack on their college members of the TKC; he elaborated on the heavy toll of souls that had wearily resulted from such a chaotic debacle.

As Vrushabh started uttering words, the glint in Rohan's eyes changed drastically from one of concern to one of disbelief and incredulity. His eyes widened in some amazement, and a little chuckle at last rolled quite suddenly from his lips, breaking the prolonged silent tension of the general atmosphere.

"Hold on, hold on, hold on," he interrupted.

"Are you meaning to say that you went to the future and saw this all happen? Were you on some drugs or what?"

He kept shaking his head very energetically from side to side to make his point.

"No, Rohan, trust me, I am absolutely off any kind of drugs! What I am telling you is the truth in its entirety. It did happen, and I need you to believe me for it."

Rohan raised his hands in a peace gesture.

"OK, OK, let's take a moment here to breathe and cool down. I believe, my friend. I genuinely do believe you."

There was no mistaking the incredulity and suspicion in his voice, but Vrushabh realised he had a long way to go in completely convincing his friend about his stance on the issue.

As they proceeded for their walk, Vrushabh knew he had to change the course of their discussion, for in this walk, he would know a method to validate the reality and legitimacy of his tale.

"Rohan," he spoke in exhilaration ",

did you know that I have been putting efforts into a mind-boggling drama that centres around the phenomenal tale of Kakbhushundi and Garuda's but?"

Rohan's eyes shot up in total surprise, absolutely caught off guard by the news.

"What? No way! How did you happen to learn about it? I haven't even had the chance to tell Abhy yet," he exclaimed, and incredulous his voice was.

Vrushabh got up with a grin; he felt an opportunity.

"That I know; for I have seen,"

replied he in a voice filled with hope.

Rohan stood like that, his eyes wide and his mouth agape in complete disbelief at what he was hearing.

"What do you mean, you've seen it? Do you mean to say that you travelled into the future and somehow happened to be present for my drama, too?"

"That's it!"

Vrushabh exclaimed, now bubbling with excitement more and more due to his revelation. "Don't you get it, Rohan? If I have that information regarding the chaos you are in, then it quite well means I really must have been to the future. Believe me, I am not lying or making it up!"

Rohan scratched his head thoughtfully; his expression said volumes: confusion laced with a dash of amusement.

"Alright, just let me make sure I understand this properly. So, you're telling me that you went into the future, saw the college being attacked and all. and now you know all about my secret drama project, which I never intended to pass on to anyone. And I am supposed to believe this fantastic story of yours?"

Vrushabh nodded vigorously and resolutely.

"Yes, Rohan! That's exactly what I am trying to tell you now. Of course, it is going to sound insane, I know. But trust me, this is the truth. I need you to trust me right now about this."

Rohan sighed deeply, as if laying the weight of his thoughts down with the exhaled breath, then shook his head gently in disbelief.

"Man, you have one hell of an imagination, don't you? To be honest, if I didn't know about this situation, I would believe you were trying to write your own dramatic story here."

Vrushabh opened his mouth to let his objections be known and thoughts be shared, but as he was about to speak, Rohan lifted his hand by way of signalling him to effectively silence him. "Look, I know you're doing your best to convince me of your point of view,

" he continued, "but, seriously, this is just too much for even you. Instead of getting caught up in this debate, how about we simply focus on enjoying the rest of our walk together, shall we?"

Vrushabh's voice boomed on the quiet road, chiding his friend Rohan, anger in his eyes, confrontational in its very purpose.

"No, we can't just be concerned with walking; we have to act and make a proper plan!"

In capital letters he was very frustrated; it was the expression of a huge weight bearing down on them. Arushi's looming threat and those of the TKC members were like a dark cloud assigned to them, shading dark shadows on their future, equally uncertain and very vague.

Rohan hesitated for that moment, feeling torn and in conflict as he stood amidst the intense forces of loyalty towards his friend and the overwhelming feeling of fear creeping into his mind.

"If you do not help me out in this critical matter of importance, then I will be left with no other option but to find a way to do it myself,"

Vrushabh continued, his resolve emanating brightly from his eyes like a beacon of hope. This was not a matter of survival; this was about the foundation of their friendship and the shared dreams and future that they dreamt with so much passion. Rohan, very conscious and aware of the gravity and the weight of the situations surrounding him, finally relented to the plea.

"Alright, my dear friend, I trust you completely,"

he replied, although with a tint of wavering uncertainty in his voice, betraying the doubts he hid deep within himself.

Both Vrushabh and Shan knew very well that the first thing to do was to gather and rally the friends around them.

"We have to persuade our friends,"

Vrushabh said because by now, a hundred thoughts had raced over his mind. As their friends gathered around them, every friend brought a unique skill, yet a piece of the puzzle that made up the bigger picture they had to complete.

They had gone through most of the challenges before, but here, this scenario that they found themselves in was quite different; this time it was bigger, and the stakes were high. Their opponent was sharper than before, clever, yet very cunning.

The noise of an excitingly electrifying atmosphere filled the moment they walked in and started the brainstorming session. He first pitched in a revolutionary thought by saying, "What if we gather everyone at the old warehouse?

It's secluded, and we can strategize without interruptions."

By this time, that sense of excitement and enthusiasm had been ignited in Vrushabh. Our once-upon-a-time laughter-rich and camaraderie-infused site, the warehouse, would now serve our purposes when it comes to a strategic hideout.

IX

Friend's united

When Vrushabh and Rohan entered the warehouse, the sky was sharply blue with an extra shining sun, and the feeling of excitement almost seemed to come alive, tangible in the atmosphere surrounding the duo. Soon enough, it was to be joined by their friends Mitesh, Abhy, Shraddha, and Devashri, each one bringing along an energy that added a lot to the atmosphere in total. A workspace usually referred to as a warehouse and related to labour did feel like it underwent a dynamic transformation into a pulsating centre of adventure and friendship.

"Alright, everyone, listen up!"

Vrushabh called excitedly, his voice thundering loud as it reverberated off the walls of the room.

"We have something extremely important to talk about that requires your full attention."

This motley crew instinctively pulled towards him, curiosity setting in and rising instantly with the urgency in his tone. Vrushabh went on to explain in detail the very difficult situation regarding TKC and Arushi, the two giants ready to throw them off their well-thought-out timeline after the upcoming fest. His words vividly painted a compelling picture of the impending chaos that loomed on the horizon, and the weight of the gravity of the situation hung palpably in the air, making everyone acutely aware of the seriousness of what lay ahead.

Abhy, the excitable one, could not hold back.

"This is like a Superman film or something! Count me in!"

His eyes shone, sparkling with the excitement of the adventure that was about to ensue as he swooped into a mock-heroic pose. Not everyone, though, shared his zeal. Mitesh, Shraddha, and Devashri exchanged hesitant glances, unsure of what they were getting into.

Feeling the air of uncertainty set in, Vrushabh turned his face towards Mitesh and gave him a piercing look.

"I know you have a thing for Devashri,"

he said as he raised his first half-face slowly to a cheeky mischievous grin. "So, if you help us with this, I will make sure that I do everything in my power to get you two together.

" Mitesh's face went wide with shock, and his expression lightened up as a cheerful, almost childishly happy, smile broke out on his face.

"Promise, really?"

he asked with great eagerness in his voice, hope and anticipation hanging heavy.

"Yeah, promise!"

Vrushabh replied and nodded to seal the deal. The atmosphere changed as Mitesh got excited and, in a jiffy, gave his consent to join them. Rohan had been watching the scene, and after this, he turned to chuckle and nudged

Vrushabh. "Well, that was easy,"

he said, impressed with the latter's prowess at motivating friends.

Abhy, at this time quite overwhelmed with the feeling of missing out on all the action and drama that seemed to be unfolding all around him, turned toward Shraddha.

"Come on, Shraddha! This is going to be nothing short of epic! We absolutely cannot let TKC and Arushi ruin our carefully crafted timeline!"

The palpable enthusiasm was infectious, and Shraddha could not help but smile—like every time the infectious energy had got the better of her, despite reservations she may have had earlier. After a little more coaxing and with adventure calling out to her, she finally agreed to join the team in this thrilling chase.

As if surging collectively with sudden enthusiasm and expectancy, Devashri broke her silence finally after watching from the fringes and soaking in the atmosphere.

"If everyone else is in, I guess I'll join too,"

she said, beaming with bright optimism. This finally sent her joining the group in a wave of relief and joy; they now felt like one team ready to take on any obstacle that was going to come their way.

As the team became one and was complete in itself, the environment within the warehouse changed dramatically from a situation of doubt to one filled with thrills and eagerness. They went on excitedly, talking about their master plan, enthusiastically brainstorming different kinds of ideas and strategies that would help them move on to success. There was laughter all around with funny tales and light-hearted jokes exchanged, and bonding grew in strength and resilience as the seconds turned into minutes.

The warehouse, once just a functional storage area for miscellaneous items, had grown into a lively haven filled with friendship and adventure. As they sat together to brainstorm what they should do and how, the special elements each member could bring forth were seen: infectious enthusiasm from Abhy, dogged determination from Mitesh, imaginative creativity from Shraddha, valuable insight from Devashri, and a keen strategic mind from Rohan. The brew of exciting adventures was mixed perfectly to create a team that would prove to be truly formidable in overcoming the challenges that lay ahead.

As the day went on and continued to unfold in beautiful ways, they did have time to share a variety of snacks and cool drinks while basking in joy from their newfound friendship. The challenges ahead of them, most of which had seemed very daunting and overwhelming, were now appearing to be much less formidable with friends by one's side through thick and thin. They pictured the approaching festival not as a celebration of what they had achieved but as a promising beginning to their epic quest to protect their timeline from any danger that might arise in it.

Rohan's heart was racing with excitement and a dash of nervousness as he gingerly congregated his closest buddies in the dark corner of the vast warehouse. The atmosphere around them was intense, brooding—murmurs of impending doom hung thick in the atmosphere, making them breathe an eerie feeling of portent among the group.

"First, Vrushabh will approach the Dean and formally request to postpone the fest,"

he began explaining in a surprisingly clear, composed tone when, in fact, his mind was swimming through a maelstrom of thoughts remorselessly.

"Why me?"

Vrushabh's voice trembled, a flicker of doubt crossing his face. Rohan leaned in closer, urgency in his tone.

"Because no one else will do it. You're our only hope."

It was a brazen plan. They would meet up at college and call the cops on them, pretending that there was some sort of emergency. While all this was going on, the unarmed but determined TKC members would confront the police, using whatever makeshift weapons we could find to confront Arushi.

Abhy, the strategist, stood up. His eyes gleamed with excitement as he surveyed the scene in front of him.

"It's perfect, down to the last-minute detail,"

he asserted confidently, underlining the fact that their planning had left nothing to chance. Then, Devashri and Shraddha exchanged a glance, and in their faces was a flicker of uncertainty and anxiety that hung like an unspoken understanding between them. Mitesh, shrouded in a haze of somnolence and fatigue, merely shrugged his shoulders when asked for his opinion—the serious implications and weight of their Byzantine scheme completely eluded him.

That day, Vrushabh geared himself up to meet Dean Das. He entered the Dean's office—the air was thick with tension.

"Sir, the college is going to be attacked during the fest,"

he blurted out, desperation lacing his words.

Mr Das furrowed his brow to indicate that he was getting irritated and replied quickly with vexation,

"I am not going to listen to such nonsense from a boy who has flunked in all his subjects."

The tone had a ring of ridicule to it, and it killed Vrushabh's earnest plea as if it were a simple, frivolous, and downright silly act.

It was an intense moment, full of a sense of heedless determination when Vrushabh boldly stepped forward with conviction and gripped the Dean's collar tightly.

"You idiot! You know what you're doing!"

he exclaimed vehemently. The words poured out of him like anything, driven by a powerful blend of fear and anger that surged within him.

Dean's eyes grew wide, his shock temporarily overtaking the furious expression that had been etched on his face just moments before.

"What are you talking about?"

he barked in an incredulous tone, but as he processed the situation, the realisation slowly began to dawn on him, illuminating the truth of the matter at hand.

Vrushabh let go reluctantly, his face twisted in a pained expression that spoke oodles for the turmoil within. It was as if the weight of the entire situation came crashing down upon him with an overwhelming force, like the crashing of waves on his confused psyche. With a sudden rush of adrenaline, he made a quick exit from the office, his heart pounding fiercely in his chest, and the echo of his own words haunting him, echoing in his mind.

Stumbling out into the night, he heaved for air as the reality of their master plan weighed in. They truly were on the brink of something monumental, caught up in a desperate gamble to save them from what they were in or prove to be the very thing that destroyed them utterly.

He came out of the dean's cabin, and like a flood, an urgency surged into him, overwhelming his senses. All around him on the campus, excitement reigned as meticulous preparation for various festivals was going on by the enthusiastic students. However, with this vibrancy of the campus, his heart was racing wildly with the unsettled feeling of dread.

"Run away as far as you can! The college is getting destroyed!"

he shouted at the very top of his voice, projecting the alarmed warning through the corridor, reverberating off the walls, reaching the ears of people nearby.

Just then, the junior standing next to him pierced through his conscience like a thorn. He felt a sharp wave of responsibility wash over him.

"Stop what you're doing right now!"

he hollered loudly, his voice carrying above the racket, while Devashri was trying hard to control the bedlam that was going on around them.

"Do not allow him to speak to the junior! The dean definitely won't take our side on the issue. What do we do in this predicament?"

Vrushabh felt a furious anger swell up inside him as if he could feel his blood race through his veins.

"What are the real chances that the police are going to listen to our concerns and take them seriously?"

he shouted back, his voice like thunder with frustration and desperation.

The weight of their precarious predicament was pressing heavily on his shoulders; he was trapped with nothing but hopeless sensations.

"You got us into this mess, and now we're all stuck here. How on earth would I know what steps to take or what to do next?"

The sudden clarity that had flashed into his mind could be compared to nothing less than a bolt of lightning, so stark was its brilliance in contrast to the surrounding obscurity. And an evermore desperate plan began to flicker and take form within the depths of his thoughts.

He immediately began to sprint out of the college campus, with an overdose of adrenaline surging through his veins and dictating every single step he made. Meanwhile, Devashri was making her way back toward Rohan. Her brow was furrowed deeply into lines of genuine concern for the situation at hand. "We definitely should have involved Sharvari in this decision-making process," she said with a tinge of regret and remorse evident in her voice.

Rohan shook his head vigorously in disapproval.

"That is a bad idea,"

He frankly expressed his thoughts.

The minutes ticked by, elongated into forever—what if they decided to do nothing at all? Devashri felt the heavy weight of choices settling onto her shoulder blades, her mind consumed by a palpable fear of the consequences that might unfold if they were to fail. Rohan's words kept echoing in her mind as a stiff reminder of their delicate and fragile alliance with each other, emphasising how important it was that they took the right course of action in this critical moment.

"Why can't we just tell someone?"

she pleaded, desperation edging into her voice.

"Because no one is going to believe us!"

Rohan finally snapped, finally losing his patience.

"It's paramount that we figure this out on our own. We simply can't involve anyone else in this complicated mess."

Devashri felt her heart sink deep into her chest, for it was weightily evident that they were all alone in this fierce and gruelling battle and the stakes at hand higher than ever before. Everywhere she saw an atmosphere so lively with the most jolly preparations going on for the upcoming festivity—the gaiety sharply contrasting with the grim and very unpromising reality of her circumstances—and she could hear laughter and feel a thick sense of excitement hanging in the air, but she could not fight off an overwhelming feeling of dread consuming her whole.

"Maybe there is a chance we can find some proof,"

she suggested, grasping at the slightest hope.

"If we can just show what is happening, maybe then we can get the help we need."

Rohan sighed and raked a hand through his hair.

"Well, what if we can't? What if we make it worse?"

The uncertainty gnawed at her relentlessly, and the feeling of unrest would not leave her mind. They were stepping into something awfully dangerous—there was no turning their backs on this precipice. And failure loomed large in her mind like a dark, black cloud about to drench her. "We have to try," she said with a voice remarkably firm and unruffled, though a maelstrom of emotions was raging inside her.

As they brainstormed on the options for what to do next, Devashri simply could not rid herself of the gnawing feeling that time was getting away from her, leaving her increasingly nervous. Her mind strayed to her best friend, Sharvari, who amazingly seemed able to extricate them from almost all challenging situations they had ever found themselves in.

"What if we just told her everything?"

she wondered aloud, thinking of a solution through Sharvari.

Rohan's gaze seemed to sharpen a little, going pointed and focused.

"And has she been embroiled in this? Not in your life, we can't let that happen. Whatever it is, we have to keep it strictly between ourselves."

The weight of secrecy was crushing her. "But what if she could help? She's smart and resourceful."

"Devashri, just think about it properly! If we involve her in all this, then we are jeopardising her life as much as ours. We definitely cannot take that sort of chance,"

spoke Rohan as his voice rose out of concern.

A single tear dropped from Devashri's eye, for the overwhelming fear of losing everything dear to her was almost too much to bear. "I don't want to see anyone hurt," she whispered, her heart heavy, filled with sorrow and deep emotional pain.

Seeing palpable fear reflected in her eyes, Rohan relented and softened. "I completely understand your feelings and concerns, but at the same time, we have to apply a degree of common sense regarding this situation. We need to ensure that our panic does not hijack our judgement and reasoning."

X

Night of the fest

Finally, the long-awaited day of the festival arrived, accompanied by excitement and zeal in the air all around. Rohan was engrossed in the extensive drama preparations by practising incessantly and brainstorming with his friends so that everything went off without a hitch. Abhy and Mitesh were busy with the implementation of their sharp and diabolic plan. They went to the police very seriously and said,

"There are goons who entered Newtech College and started beating up students."

To this, their plan was embroiled in prompt urgency from the police, and at that moment, they were satisfactorily elated and victorious, thinking without an ounce of doubt that their plan did work out.

They both rushed; immense joy was boiling up within them, as they needed to convey to Devashri and Shraddha the interest that was mixing into the wonderful festivities all around. As they threaded through the surging and vibrant crowd, engrossed with palpable feelings of anticipation and celebration, they happened to come across Sharvari, who was elegantly manoeuvring her way through the crowd in a wheelchair, exuding an unfathomable sense of grace and determination into the bargain, faithfully guided by her loving grandma. The more delightful it was for them to see her, the rays of happiness shone brighter for them to the highest peaks.

In a fit of excitement and eagerness, Shraddha, in a belatedly excited gesture, inadvertently spilt juice all over Sharvari's clothes, creating a bit of a mess.

"Oh no! I am so sorry!"

Shraddha exclaimed, turning red as she felt the onset of a wave of embarrassment. But then, Sharvari, with a warm and reassuring smile lighting up her face, comforted her by saying,

"It's okay; it's just juice and will wash out without hassle."

So, what had started as an embarrassing moment turned into a shared laugh between two friends, lightening the atmosphere around them and putting the joy back into the interaction?

As the long-awaited drama was to start shortly, the eager group was heading towards the great auditorium, throbbing within for a sense of thrill and anticipation. The atmosphere around was electric and they could feel their hearts pounding in rapture as they moved towards the place. But going unobserved by the rest of the group, Sharvari and her grandma quickly slipped into the restroom to powder their noses and be prepared so that they would not miss a single moment of the show.

Inside the large auditorium, Rohan stood backstage, as he had always harnessed the imagination to do, ready to come out onto the stage. As the lights dimmed slowly, an electric surge of anticipation built in the audience and filled the atmosphere thick with expectation. Rohan's heart swelled with pride, thinking about how much toil and hard work was invested in framing this drama. These friends standing with him at this moment did not just consist of fellow companions in the drama but formed a tightly-knit family through their affiliation toward performance art.

Mr. Kulkarni's voice reverberated across the auditorium, manufacturing an unusual, peculiar mix of commanding authority and indefinable urgency that enveloped everyone present in its sweep.

"Just now, my phone rang. It was from a dear friend of mine, a police officer, who apprised me of the fact that a gang of ruffians had attacked our college premises. Do you have any information about it?"

His eyes, filled with deep concern, surveyed the room for Mitesh and Abhy, who were visibly holding and exchanging worried glances, taken aback by the shocking information.

"No, Sir, we don't know anything at all,"

stammered out Mitesh in a voice very nervous, and beads of sweat formed and accumulated on his brow as anxiety surged within. The tension in the room thickened immensely; it was so thick that one could cut it with a knife, and Mr. Kulkarni's face turned ominously dark. "Irrational, just like you, Vrushabh? Has your brain stopped functioning?" he snapped in a sharp tone, frustration clear and quite unmistakable in the shell-shocked tone of his.

Mitesh, cornered and somewhat trapped, hastened to respond, "I am sorry, sir. We shall inform the police about what has happened and accept our mistake in its entirety." But before he could say anything further, Mr. Kulkarni cut him sharp with his tone as he said,

"There is no need for that. I have already taken the initiative of telling the authorities that no such incident has taken place."

The weight of the sentence hung in the atmosphere, leaving both Mitesh and Abhy acutely aware of just how heavy their situation was.

Realising that all their well-laid plans were shattering into pieces in front of their eyes, they ran backstage hastily in search of Rohan. The speed of their movements was perfectly synchronised with the mounting panic stirring within their bosoms. On seeing Rohan, they quickly broke the news about the police and how it had caught them unawares. Rohan's mind, now reeling under the pressure of the situation, began working on a quick solution.

"You need to go and find Devashri and Shraddha immediately. We have to ensure that all the entrances of the auditorium are closed from the outside,"

he urgently instructed, his voice refusing to crack against the surrounding din and anarchy.

Having, thus, discovered the collective resolve and urgency of the situation, they rushed toward the multiple exits of the auditorium to see each one was firmly closed.

Their heartbeat was racing against the rapidity of their breaths, echoing the depth of the moment. As they carefully locked each door, one after the other, the brazen realisation of their dicey situation began to sink more profoundly: they were trapped in a situation of their own making. Panic-stricken, they tried frantically to contact Vrushabh, but his mobile phone only rang, and they could not get any response, which intensified the tension and discomfort already building among them.

What once was an auditorium full of life and vibrancy, surrounded by learning and laughter, seemed more of a cage that closed in with its oppressiveness. Shadows danced across the walls, draping everything in an eerie ambience as whispers of uncertainty and doubt wrapped around them. Mitesh, Abhy, and Rohan exchanged nervous glances at one another as each man's thoughts deeply clung to the possibilities that might occur from actions and decisions, weighing the outcomes ahead.

With minutes turning endless, uneasiness and discomfort became visible on Mitesh's face. The unending and threatening silence of Vrushabh and many unanswered calls contributed to the ever-growing apprehension, anxiety, and worry. As the seconds ticked by, the hope of Arushi and TKC's arrival finally showing up started winning over, depressing the whole group and shadowing bad omens all over.

It was a shared experience as Rohan, Shraddha, and Devashri felt Mitesh's rising anxiety, with their nerves already frayed and stretched taut by the overwhelming uncertainty that surrounded them. This information that Vrushabh had given them earlier now carried an ominous weight, much like a ticking time bomb counting down to an event they all felt so unprepared to meet. The tension hung in the air, thick enough that one could almost cut it with a knife, every breath heavy with anticipation of unknown possibilities lying ahead of them.

Abhy, at the main gate, had his high vigil eyes on the far horizon, vigilant for the slightest signal of the expected arrival of Arushi and TKC. Indeed, a great amount of responsibility weighed down his shoulders, as he knew their coming could turn everything upside-down in one second and change everything drastically. With the passing of every vehicle, his heart used to race, pounding with excitement and anxiety as his mind continuously envisioned a host of situations, some of them being quite propitious and positive and others extremely bad and disconcerting.

The silence that had fallen within the room was so deep and overwhelming that it easily could be described as deafening, punctuated only by the occasional creak of a floorboard beneath him or the very faint and distant hum of traffic that could be heard far away. Mitesh found himself adrift in a maze of complicated thoughts and reflections, each proving to be even more unsettling and troubling than the last, leading him deeper into a state of confusion. Continuing to dwell on these unfolding events that were leading him to this particular moment, he replayed in his mind every single detail, looking fervently for any clue, any kind of subtle hint to give insight into the confounding situation that faced him now.

Rohan, Shraddha, and Devashri had bunched up and were whispering so softly it could hardly be heard by those around them. They were very well aware that their fate was as unpredictable as the people around them and the decisions they took. The fragility of the situation made this already strong feeling of being vulnerable even stronger. They yearned for Vrushabh's comforting presence under such a tense situation, who would help to provide relief and company with his boundless guidance during adverse situations, thus adding security to their strength.

Abhy's adrenaline surged as he saw armour-clad figures. "They must be the TKC!" Abhy screamed and rushed to meet his friends. Rohan and others quickly pick up their weapons, while Mitesh creates a diversion by throwing firecrackers with loud pops that reverberate through the tension in the air.

Abhy gladly took advantage of the opportunity that came his way by throwing a smoke bomb he had prepared himself towards Arushi. The bomb exploded and surrounded her in thick, dense smoke. Her surroundings changed abruptly, and she spun around in a state of bewilderment. Rohan suddenly lunged toward her with a cricket bat in hand, hoping to knock her out with one decisive blow.

But Arushi showed all the agility and wildness of an animal that had fallen into a precarious position and dispatched a powerful kick square on Rohan's face, smashing him powerfully to the ground. She came back with a dash of aggression on both of them for the unexpected attack she was under, smacking Abhy vigorously with blood pouring down from his nose as she brandished her gun to create a scene that seemed as though history was playing its rerun once again.

Just when she was going to pull the trigger, with everything in place, a bullet whizzed past her at amazing velocity, knocking the gun forcefully out of her hand and clattering it to the ground. She turned her head sideways to view this unexpected development, seeing her younger self standing there, flanked by a group of her gang members all attired in stylish black outfits, with Vrushabh noticeably upfront. Their timely intervention not only drastically shifted the tide of the encounter but also exploded into an intense, chaotic battle that broke out between the two rival factions.

The members of the TKC regrouped; the atmosphere was charged with an almost palpable tension. This ragtag group of men stood tall against the chaotic backdrop that surrounded it, imposingly armoured. Abhy, Rohan, and Mitesh flashed urgent, full-of-concern looks at one another, knowing quite well by then how quickly the situation had escalated beyond what they had planned initially. The thickening smoke, heavy with the smell of acrid soot and metallic tang of blood, heightened their senses about the dangerous circumstances they were in.

Arushi, fueled by a convoluted mix of fear and sheer determination, stood resolute as she faced her younger self. There she was, appearing in front of her like a reflection of herself in time.

"You don't comprehend the magnitude of what you're getting into!"

she screamed at the top of her lungs, her voice barely above the noise and chaos that surrounded them. Smirking with an air of superiority, the younger Arushi returned her ridicule, radiating confidence so thick it was almost palpable.

"I know fully well what I am doing, no doubt about it. It is you who looks completely lost," she responded with a tone of confidence.

Clash with the time keeping commission

That was a bright night, as if the horrible battle between the TKC, and the strong men of Young Arushi's group had ignited fire in the sky. Vrushabh found the quickest gait he could toward all his closest friends, all involved in a great fight with the TKC members: Rohan and Abhy Reaching their side in the tumult, he asked quickly,

"Where are Shraddha and Devashri?"

while he picked Abhy up from the ground and also handed him a napkin to clean the blood streaming from his nose, which seemed to be cut.

Vrushabh's actions came as a shock to Rohan, who winced in pain as he pulled at his hair, asking,

"What did you do?"

Vrushabh replied,

"I promised her I would return the package. The actual trick was finding her."

Abhy was taken aback, and from incredulity, he asked,

"She agreed to just that?"

To this, Vrushabh responded, saying,

"She did, to be real with you."

In a slick confrontation, resounding across the shadows, was the future version of Arushi, locked in combat with her younger self. The two Arushis hurled hand-to-hand combat at each other; movement became a blur of pace and agility, shrouded in darkness upon the college campus. While Mitesh and Shraddha took the critical responsibility of dealing with the firecrackers, they relentlessly attacked with a barrage of explosive projectiles directed at both the TKC and Arushi.

The legendary fight between the notorious gang of TKC and their rivals was boiling with a whole new level of violence, to which Vrushabh, along with others, thought it was time to join hands with their allies Mitesh, Shraddha, and Devashri to stand as one.

The atmosphere around them was heavy and electric, with the ear-deafening sounds of a clash of weapons against each other and the sharp crackle of firecrackers adding to the hallowed chaos that surrounded the scene.

Feeling the thump of his racing heart pound within his chest, Vrushabh took a deep breath to steady himself before charging headlong into the melee. As he entered the tumult, he skillfully dodged a powerful swing from a TKC member's baton aimed at him, barely missing the impact, and followed it immediately with a quick, well-placed kick at the opponent's shin.

The TKC member stumbled backwards in surprise and pain, opening up a gap just enough to allow Vrushabh to plunge into a flurry of punches that landed squarely in the belly of his opponent.

Vrushabh's extraordinary bravery inspired Rohan so much that he felt determination and courage rushing through his veins, forcing him to join the fight.

He picked up a fallen baton from the ground and started swinging it skillfully with all his might at the oncoming TKC members, knocking them back one by one without a miss. Abhy, too, did not hesitate to join his friends in the fight despite the pain caused by his bleeding nose; he relied on his superb agility to evade incoming attacks but also made sure to land strategic blows whenever an opportunity presented itself.

Shraddha and Devashri worked in perfect unison, advancing as one so their fireworks exploded resoundingly on all sides of the TKC to disorient them, while concurrently creating opportunities for haymakers to be connected by their gang. Mitesh, his face set in determined lines, launched fireworks quite accurately at the weak points of the TKC to achieve maximum effect.

In every move she made, the graceful and powerful future Arushi dodged and parried every strike her smaller self meted out. The two Arushis danced an elegant ballet, beautiful and deadly, with fists and feet blurred together as they shifted in and out of the blackness of the night.

The young Arushi, whose eyes were wide open with fear and confusion, struggled to keep up with the superb display of skill and experience her older counterpart was showing.

As if the scene around them wasn't chaotic enough, with all that transpiring, a hormone-crazed member of the Time Keeping Commission brandished a disintegrating club, ready to launch an aggressive attack against the firecrackers adding to the commotion.

Crackling energy filled the air, and just as he was about to unleash his weapon, Sharvari suddenly appeared from a nearby door, her grandmother carefully guiding her wheelchair forward. Suddenly, a stray bit of debris cut through the air and struck the TKC member, and he lost his precarious balance, inadvertently hurling the cube toward Sharvari and disrupting the atmosphere even further.

In this quite fantastic and unexpected display of heroism, another brave member of TKC suddenly leapt into the chaotic fray, gallantly positioning himself between the dangerous cube and helpless Sharvari. For a heart-stopping moment, the cube exploded violently upon impact, thus disintegrating him immediately and completely. Briefly, the gesticulating moment froze—congealing the ghastly scene in its eerie stillness—as disbelief rippled off the witnesses. Rohan, there to see this wonderfully selfless act, couldn't help but blurt in amazement,

"Who could somehow want to destroy our timeline by saving lives? What does it mean?"

Indeed, he was clouded by a very thick fog of confusion as his nervous eyes skimmed through the faces before him in search of answers to the overwhelming questions swirling in his mind.

The air hung tangibly heavy-laden, filled with a sense of uncertainty as if the remnants of the TKC member's deep sacrifice hung palpably. Rohan's thoughts raced in a surge that was overwhelming as his mind wrestled vigorously with the deep implications such a striking contradiction presented. Could this remarkable act of bravery be an outward indicator of some deeper war brewing within the ranks that made up the TKC? Or could it somehow be construed as a desperate cry for redemption from someone once belonging to the very forces bent on disrupting and destabilising their timeline?

It was shocking, yet she realised she was unharmed. The scene before her was one of bedlam. In her mind, firecrackers that had been simple emblems of joyous celebration now appeared as portentous harbingers of potential destruction.

It was almost impossible to process the whirlwind of contradictory emotions whirring inside her—fear clutching at their heart, gratitude for her safety flooding her mind, and a budding sense of purpose taking root deep inside. Her grandmother's soft squeeze of her hand gave her a sense of grounding from the overwhelming turmoil, softly whispering words of reassurance that wrapped around Sharvari like a warm blanket.

Slowly, the dust began to settle around them, and Rohan walked a few steps toward Sharvari; his eyes met directly with hers.

"We have to understand why he did that," he stated firmly but totally in a very even, soft tone despite all of the chaos around him.

"If they have people in the TKC ready to die for our cause, then that changes everything for us.".

The other TKC members exchanged looks, a mixture of incredulity and deep thoughts on the situation at hand. Could it be that the very organisation set up to oversee the fabric of time itself was developing cracks and fissures from within its very own ranks? Rohan's provoking question hung in the atmosphere like a heavy, weighty feeling, laden with profound possibilities.

The relative silence that had filled the area for a second was shattered out of the blue by an extremely loud boom of the firecracker, returning everybody's attention to the chaotic battlefield. At that very moment, fireworks went off in an extremely breathtaking and truly amazing display of colours against the pitch-black sky, illuminating it with brilliance and vibrancy. Exhilarating but terrifying, this overwhelming cacophony arising from the explosive display sent adrenaline rushing through the veins—it was only a subtle reminder of how high the stakes were in this precarious situation.

Knowing that victory wasn't very far and it was almost near their grasp, Vrushabh called all his close friends together, and they started planning with precision how to get back the keys of the time machine from the hold of Arushi. The ambience surrounding them was just electric, every heartbeat almost thumping loudly in their ears with the excitement and the thrill of what, no doubt, soon would be looming victorious for them.

Rohan was trapped deep into the labyrinth of his thoughts, thinking about the strange and unusual act of a person holding charge in the TKC who had done the deed of saving Sharvari from her fate. What could be the reason behind such a surprising act in the wake of all the chaos mushrooming around her?

Shraddha and Devashri had managed to expertly and finally relocate with Sharvari and her grandmother to a significant vantage point, not only free from the disturbances of the surrounding commotion but also not completely out of sight of the raging battle that was taking place. The tension was almost palpable as the four of them took their position, casting glances from the warring warriors in combat to the time machine, so integral and central to their plan.

With a powerful mix of unwavering conviction and desperate urgency, two rival factions readied themselves for an imminent clash. The TKC members wore intimidating dark uniforms and had an air about them that was somewhat menacing, with fierce determination burning like live coals in their eyes and promising to take on anything at any time. At the other end of this contrast stood Vrushabh's team, brimming with fierce and resolute spirit and wholeheartedly bound together by every member's sense of purpose and dedicated service toward their cause.

The moment of confrontation, so long awaited, burst through the cacophony with a deafening roar that reverberated through the very space of the battlefield. All of a sudden, the environment had turned into a circus of pandemonium and commotion. The sky was filled with shouting, crying, metal clashing against metal, each strike deep with the unbearable heaviness of cost at stake in this unforgiving contest.

Amidst the rough and tumble that was developing en masse, Vrushabh's speed of thought raced on full throttle while working on planning the next strategic move to make amidst all this disorder. If, at this point, they could just get hold of the keys, that would enable them to send TKC right back to their point of inception and end the evil plans here and now.

Remaining FLOCKED-IN FINISHED WITH THE hitherto raging and indecently fierce battle around him, Rohan's thoughts kept coming back to the momentous and seminal decision that had been taken by a member of the TKC to save Sharvari. He could not help but wonder: was this supposed to be a challenge thrown by one of their members against them, or did it stand for some amazingly deep realisation of what was at stake at this point? That inner conflict gnawed pitilessly at his mind, driving away his concentration from the battle currently engaged and causing him to doubt everything he thought he knew.

Shraddha and Devashri watched with bated breaths from the haven, worried glances exchanged between them, riddled with concern and fear. They were more than aware of what the time machine was to them; it wasn't just a tool that could help in escaping the situation they now found themselves in, but a mute symbol of the fight for survival that continued unabated, the keys in their hands towering as the last bastion of light in the aura of darkness and uncertainty surrounding them.

With every moment that ticked past, the tide of battle ebbed and flowed in ways that no one could predict, increasingly appearing that the eventual outcome of this brutal confrontation was anything but guaranteed. The members of TKC fought with a type of ferocity born of great despair, their movements flowing seamlessly together in a fluid, exact opposition to their enemies. For reasons much the same, Vrushabh's team—though impassioned and dedicated—struggled substantially at keeping themselves together and maintaining a level of cohesion and unity under the relentless attack that they had faced.

With a raging battlefield at her side, future Arushi felt the weight of impending defeat exceedingly pressing down her shoulders. Enraged, she surged up, and from that surge, a fire was born that could no longer be contained or suppressed. She dug deep into her pocket, feeling the fabric her fingers brushed against, to bring out a mysterious cube like an aura intrigue. It glowed ominously in her hand, pulsing with vibrant energy—palpable as it began to spin at incredible speed, creating a mesmerising vortex of light that captivated her attention, alongside that of all else around her.

She now launched a strong kick, squarely aimed at her younger self. Her determination was unbending and fierce, enough to serve as both a grave warning and an urgent catalyst for transformative change. Immediately after doing so, she picked up the cube and flung it with all her might toward the chaotic fray in which young Arushi's gang was violently clashing with the members of the TKC.

The cube moved tastefully through the air, leaving behind a mesmerising display of brilliant sparks that shimmered and danced in its wake before it finally detonated in an overwhelming and blinding light. An explosion unlike anything anybody had ever seen, not only did it disintegrate the gang members caught in its ferocious blast, but it even claimed half of her forces in an instant and left behind nothing but haunting echoes of anguished screams ringing through the air.

Turning towards Vrushabh and his bunch of friends, future Arushi stood amidst the complete and utter destruction that had unfolded all around her; her expression reflected a strange and chilling mix of pure anger and grim satisfaction.

Streaks of blood on her face simply stood as an epitome of the overpowering chaos and turmoil that surrounded her then. She donned a bone-chilling smile on her lips, saying, "You are the first to hassle me so much." The words were laced with venom as they came out, and the heavy silence that remained after the explosion carried that voice ominously.

It was then that the remains of the pit that fight that had just ensued quieted down, and the air surrounding them began to smoulder in an electric tension as all their eyes were now locked on the single figure standing before them—the potential harbinger of destruction, Future Arushi.

Her eruption with auras did not lack the tingle necessary to evoke terror and awe in any adversary who ran into her sights. Her piercing eyes could pass through the smoke and dust floating here and there, not missing even a shred of Vrushabh, stone-frozen in shock at not understanding what had happened.

XII

The night finally ended

As Arushi bravely stepped into the frenzy, a powerful surge of adrenaline rush coursed through her veins, electrifying her senses. Vrushabh and Abhy were running towards her with tightly clenched fists, their intentions ominous and full of threats. She nimbly turned to the side, dodging their aggressive blows with great skill as her well-honed instincts came into action. Before one could blink one's eyes, she swiftly drew her gun from its holster—the cold metal feeling like a reassuring weight firmly nestled in her hand.

With an aim unfaltering and sure, she fired her gun; the bullet streaked through the air with precision and struck Abhy, causing a sickening thud that echoed back at them from all around. He crumpled to the ground in a second, his eyes wide open in shock and incredulity; a final gasp of life escaped his lips and was lost to the air around.

The silence that followed was deafening, stomach-churning, and utterly all-consuming; it was broken only by Shraddha's anguished, heart-wrenching scream that pierced sharply through the heavy atmosphere.

"No!"

she cried despairingly, the voice breaking under the weight of her grief as she saw the love of her life slipping away from her grasp, his light of life ebbing gradually from his eyes, and leaving her utterly devastated.

Vrushabh stood in a frozen attitude, his face contorted in a look of unadulterated horror, as vivid memories of a previous timeline came flooding in with overwhelming force. Past blunders echoed voluminously inside; each moment was a poignant reminder of how everything could spiral into chaos and fall apart completely in a jiffy. He felt the weight of inevitability hard on his head, that creepy feeling of déjà vu which left him gasping for breath and fumbling to keep up with the feelings piling up inside.

"Vrushabh, come here fast!"

His voice crept through the hazy atmosphere with the sort of urgency that had seeped into it, commanding and impossible to ignore. The razor-like sharpness of the sound jolted him abruptly back to the present moment, pulling him from his deep reverie. He turned around without a second thought and instinctively ran back towards the comforting safety of his friends.

The overwhelming chaos behind him gradually faded into the background, becoming a far-away memory.

He could feel the fast beating of his heart as he sprinted with all of his might, each rhythmic beat pounding back to remind him just how big the stakes were in this predicament. In one motion, the group circled tightly together, fear and naked resolution etched on every face.

They huddled closer, urgently strategizing at hand what next move lay ahead—well aware that the danger was far from resolved, much less behind them.

Rohan's voice barely left him as he reiterated to Vrushabh the weight of their circumstance.

"Sharvari is indispensable to us,"

he said, going back to the way the latter was taken when the timeline had broken down—something that felt too purposeful for their ends of destruction. "Hm. But why risk everything to save her?"

said Vrushabh; his mind was running at top speed.

"Well, I think I have an idea of it,"

Rohan said with narrowed eyes, thinking over the implications.

"She helped build the time dilator and is a critical part of building it. That explains why she's valuable. If an adjustment were to be made to it with her equation, we would indeed be setting sail through time itself. And that's beside the point—she's in love with you, even though she seems to deny it. She knows deep within that you are worth so much more than the shortcomings she's willing to suffer just because she's using a wheelchair."

The realisation hit Vrushabh like a ton of bricks, and suddenly his mind started racing with jumbled thoughts; it felt as if all of Rohan's powerful words had hit him at once, making him unable to focus for one second. Deep inside, he knew he had to work differently—not just for Sharvari but for all of them as a group. With a greater sense of purpose welling up inside him, he moved forward—determination alighting inside him afresh like a fierce flame.

He faced his future Arushi in a highly apprehensive moment of tension, holding his gun tight in hand, with Sharvari equally resolute by his side. The tension around them sizzled hot; the importance of the situation was loud with every echoing beat of the heart.

He stood making his epic choice: whether he would save Sharvari to change their fate together or if this single decision would make all of them move godsward toward ultimate doom and despair. The suspense was hanging thick in the air like dense fog, which was pushing him forward inch by inch into a dark, uncertain destiny ahead of him.

Vrushabh's hands were shaking uncontrollably with anxiety and anticipation while he carefully tore open the package, and inside, right in front of him, was a sleek, menacing black gun. Taking his heart to his chest, he pointed the weapon at the future version of Arushi, who was standing there confident, mocking, with laughter, "Do you even know how to use a gun?

"No, I don't,"

he confessed, a shade diffidently, indeed, for the weapon seemed in his grasp like a ponderous extraneousness.

He suddenly wheeled the gun toward Sharvari, who was standing just a few feet away from him. A frantic scream emerged from Arushi as she yelped, "No!" The urgency and desperation buried in her voice echoed through the dimly lit room, making the air cold. She knew how critical and crucial the moment was; after all, it wasn't just another person—she was the keystone of all timelines, intertwined with which they were living.

The TKC head had warned her that Sharvari's death, caused by anything other than a predestined event, would unravel the Time Keeping Commission (TKC). It was a fragile balance, one that kept time itself in check. If Sharvari fell, the consequences would ripple through every timeline, leading to chaos.

Arushi's mind raced back to the equation she had deciphered, the one that pointed to this very moment. Each variable was crucial, and Sharvari was the constant that anchored them all. The future depended on her survival.

"Drop it, Vrushabh!" Arushi urged, her voice pleading with him with a level of desperation that portrayed the intensity of that moment.

Vrushabh's eyes, however, were wild and rampant with a storm of confusion and fear.

"I don't want to hurt anyone!"

he cried out, his voice nearly cracking due to an emotional overload. "But I just absolutely cannot let you take her away from me!

"Take her away? You don't understand the magnitude of it all!"

Arushi pleaded fervently, stepping closer to drive her point across, hands raised in a very humanly sincere gesture for peace and calm.

"You pull that trigger, and everything you know and hold dear changes right there in that second. You'll condemn us all to an uncertain fate!"

The air was so taut that one would have thought it had physically wrapped itself thick, like fog, around all the people present. There she stood, immobile, fear in her eyes overwhelming and ready to spill out, yet carrying with it, buried deep, a glimmer of realisation. Deep down, she knew her role, her importance in the workings of time, and how this knowledge tortured her mind and heart.

The sudden drop of the gun made Future Arushi's heart race in her chest as she came to grips with the moment that unfolded in front of her.

"Will I surrender?"

she asked herself confidently, but her quivering voice betrayed her uncertainly and showed her fear.

"Please, just don't hurt Sharvari,"

she pleaded with Vrushabh again and again as he stood unflinching and unbudging, his determination and resolution clear in the air around them. "I know what I need to do,

" he declared firmly, loading the gun with a calmness that sent shivers down her spine.

In a fleeting second that seemed to transcend time, Arushi's future self came flying towards him, fast enough that everything around her became a blur, but this was suddenly halted when she reached her younger version, whose eyes conveyed some sort of intensity and desperation.

"Stop this!"

she shrieked in a voice that cut through the pandemonium, but the urgency and seriousness of what was going on around them proved simply too pressing.

Vrushabh turned to Sharvari, his eyes locking onto hers, and softly said,

"Please give up your dream of being a physicist."

There were tones of heavy feelings in the air. She fired back at him:

"It's the only thing that gives meaning to my useless life,"

defying him with her light, angry eyes.

"I'll give you everything you want,"

he replied, his voice level but laced with emotions so profound, unmistakable.

"You are the thought that I wake up to in the morning, the beautiful dream that lingers in my mind as I sleep at night. And if the timelines cannot find a way to forget you, then let me be forgotten with you."

"But you very well know that I cannot be yours,"
Sharvari said, her voice shaking as tears started welling up in her eyes.

"I understand,"
he said, his voice dripping with painful acknowledgement.

"I beg of you, just fulfil this last desire of mine if you will: please do not go ahead and create the equation."

His words were futile, a flat noise within the mess of confusion that surrounded them. The mood within the room changed greatly, from completely under control to unbearable, and it was within this that Vrushabh stood and pointed the gun to his head.

For a brief moment, he looked at the face of Shraddha, then at Mitesh, then Rohan, and, finally at Devashri, taking note of the expression of deep despair that had taken over their faces. "Respect at least my last wish," he said very softly, "and remember, my name is Vrushabh Patankar."

The trigger clicked decisively with a deafeningly loud bang across the entirely serviced space, and he dramatically collapsed to the ground in a heap. This impulsive act sent ripples of shock powerfully across the room, setting an atmosphere so thick with tension, and then Arushi, along with the TKC members, vanished into thin air as if they had never existed. The rest of the friends came rushing towards Vrushabh in urgency, their faces a cascade of sorrow and despair, streaming with tears, while Devashri stood frozen to the floor, the moment of horror overwhelming her senses and rendering her momentarily paralyzed.

As the doors of the auditorium swung wide open, there was a sense of urgency as the group rushed forth in a desperate attempt to liberate the students who were still trapped inside. Their hearts were weighed down with an overwhelming sense of grief and despair.

Rohan, feeling the immense burden of loss from his dear friend, stepped out tentatively into the cool night air, heavy with sorrow and anguish, as if the very darkness around was mimicking the turmoil inside him.

Meanwhile, Sharvari raised her eyes to the vastness of the night sky and bravely battled the tears that were about to spill down her cheeks. Stars are shown above, indifferent to the scorching pain she was going through at that very moment.

Yet, she felt an unusual, deep connection to the surrounding universe. Each star seemed softly to whisper secrets of lost dreams, of vows that had remained unredeemed, in the silent night.

Then all that could be felt in the aftermath was thick, eery despair. His friends closed in around Vrushabh's lifeless body and their wrenching sobs bounced off the walls of the empty auditorium. If they were united in grief, then each of them was his island of sorrow and remembrance, applying the specifics of that shock in their way.

As they grieved, it flashed in their minds: the laughter and shared dreams. Rohan reminisced about the late-night study sessions, the shared ambitions, and promises of a bright future. Now, shattered dreams had replaced those, replaced with a feeling of overwhelming loss.

It was then that Devashri finally summoned up the courage to break her long silence, her voice trembling with the weight of the emotions.

"We should have done something. We could have saved him,"

she said, her words filled with regret and sorrow. The others nodded in agreement, expressions reflective of the gnawing guilt within. All felt completely impotent to do anything at all against being caught in a maze of fears and indecisiveness that prevented them from acting.

She took a step forward, her voice very soft, barely audible to the people standing around her.

"He believed in me, in everything that I wanted to achieve, my dreams, and my ambitions. I just cannot let his sacrifice be in vain, without purpose."

That undying spirit within her lit a small but important fire amongst the people collected there. They realized that they needed to do something worthwhile in the memory of Vrushabh to make sure that they were able to preserve the legacy he had left.

The night air enveloped them as they emerged from the auditorium, heavy, yet vibrantly charged with a deep sense of purpose. They agreed not to let despair attack and consume them completely. On the contrary, they would actively choose to turn their profound sorrow into something meaningful so that through their Collectively composite efforts and determination, the dreams and aspirations of Vrushabh shall live on.

Within a few days, they got together with the firm resolve to start a foundation in his memory that would work for the support of young physicists. They engaged in various activities and shared stories, raising awareness about mental health to prevent a similar tragedy from occurring to others.

Many a night did Sharvari stare up into the sky, and in that limitless expanse of darkness, she felt the irrepressible presence of Vrushabh. It is in these deeply silent moments that she whispered her deepest hopes and dreams out loud into the cosmos above; somewhere, she believed he was listening to these confessions.

And each tear that fell from her eyes became a telling story of her love that he always remained the embodiment of, evoking the bittersweet memories of the indelible bond that they shared in this life.

This deep sorrow and grief thus worked as a very powerful driving force for great change in the community because of their unified and collaborative effort. Indeed, the foundation did not just survive but did so spectacularly, inspiring generations upon generations of young minds to boldly pursue passions and dreams just as Vrushabh had so wholesomely encouraged Sharvari to do many times in the past.

As the night of the fest finally ended everyone was relieved as there was no battle to fight for the timeline and they where to begin the usual as they used to be before.